The First Day of Us

The First Day of Us

LISA KEIFER

First paperback edition November 2020

Cover Design by Brenda Camp Walter, Blue Valley Author Services

ISBN 978-0-578-69878-6

www.lisakeiferauthor.com

To my darling husband, I will forever hold in my heart our first day together

Chapter One

A booming voice echoed out to me as I quickly made my way down the corridor. "As I said, the headline in every print ad must *firmly* grab the reader's attention!"

During my half-jog/half-sprint—as I weaved my way around people, hoping I wouldn't knock them over—several monotonous voices emanated out to me from different meeting rooms while others, such as Headline Man, were much more animated. I was rushing to find my next seminar, which had started ten minutes earlier. This was okay with me, though. More than okay, actually, because I didn't want to be at this stupid conference, anyway.

Well, it was okay at first. When I left the previous workshop, I had zero intention of hurrying, even knowing I'd be late. Then I thought of my boss. My rather frightening, always demanding boss Mari. Just thinking of her name sped up my breathing. As a twenty-five-year-old copywriter for Madison Advertising in Chicago, I was no stranger to significant tension, but Mari, our Creative Director, took it to a whole new level.

"Disappointing, Christabel," I recalled her saying to me the previous day about honestly flawless work. *"Disappointing."* Then she clicked her tongue and rolled her eyes before stalking away. This was only a sample of the agony she often put me and others through.

I nearly slammed into an older woman carrying a large red tote bag filled to the brim with pamphlets and brochures. By the time I reached the designated conference room, I was fifteen minutes late—a new record for me. I was never more than five minutes late for anything work-related, even when it was something I felt this much disgust for.

I was often late for other things, however. It wasn't for a lack of trying to be on time, either, nor was it intentional in any way. Sometimes, I felt like the harder I tried to be on time or even (gasp!) *early*, the later I ended up. I had no idea what that was about.

The frantic, million-miles-an-hour thing was how I felt at the advertising conference. I was scrambling around an unfamiliar building, lost in a maze of identically boring hallways and identically boring rooms. I was in such a frenzied rush that I nearly missed the correct door. Then I got a text on my phone, which I ignored.

Luckily, neither the instructor nor Mari seemed to notice my tardiness as I crept into the room and took a seat at the back. Everyone in this class appeared interested in the presentation. Or at least they pretended to be.

I received another text before I'd been in the room two minutes. My phone was on vibrate, thankfully, because Mari would have ripped into me for not turning off my phone. I quickly looked at the screen. It was a text from Logan, my boyfriend.

Logan: Dinner?
Me: Can't. Conference.
Logan: Oops. Forgot.
Seriously? I told him about this conference five times the previous week and twice the day before. Who forgets after that? I stashed my phone in my purse and focused on the instructor.

This most recent class was all about online banner ads. It was a topic I knew all about and also one that brought up bad memories of a client from the first time I'd worked on a banner advertisement. It was a nightmare campaign, to say the least.

When the forty-five-minute-long workshop was over, I'd learned very little and daydreamed through the rest. I had already suspected that whoever put together this particular seminar lazily selected their instructors off random web searches instead of from any certified associations. I couldn't believe how appallingly everything else had been arranged, either.

This place was a maze of dead-end corridors, unnumbered rooms, and mismatched décor. With all the clashing colors, nothing stood out enough to be distinguished from anything else. Even the guide maps we had didn't match the layout in the building.

I was so embarrassed for this place that I couldn't see myself recommending it to anyone. I just couldn't. It was too awful.

I headed down the hall, chatting with a few of my co-workers who had recently exited other courses in the same area. One of them, my dearest work friend and fellow copywriter, Jetta, had heard Mari complaining earlier that day about the gross simplicity of the seminars. "I don't think she expected it to be so easy for us. She said sending us here was like sending us back to kindergarten."

"I don't know why she thought it would be more challenging," I replied. "I saw one of the flyers they sent out about this thing. It wasn't that great. More fluff than anything. Nothing intelligent. Nothing witty. I doubt any self-respecting copywriter created it."

I almost shuddered at the memory of that flyer. Maybe the creator didn't have nightmares from it, but I sure did. It certainly didn't inspire confidence in those of us who had a thorough understanding of our professions.

"Did Mari look at it?" Alissa, another copywriter from our agency, asked. She had more of a compassionate nature as far as Mari was concerned. However, her kindness and naiveté made this easier to forgive.

Jetta shrugged her dark brown shoulders, her sleeveless dress a juxtaposition to the cold air around us in the poorly ventilated corridor. "She had to. We're here, aren't we?" Her tone was casual and indifferent, but I knew better than to trust that.

"I heard Mari explaining to someone on the phone that she can't have her staff looking like they don't know what they're doing. She wants 'her staff' to be better than anyone else's. As if she was the one who hired us or something," I couldn't help but add with bitterness.

Joe, Alissa's boyfriend and a copywriter on her team, grumbled, "If she'd take her head out of her own ass for a second, she'd realize we're better than the rest."

Jetta laughed, then turned to me. "Did Mari even read the descriptions of these stupid courses?" I shrugged as she continued. "We might as well have returned to kindergarten. I'm sure that would have been more challenging."

"She treats us like we're imbeciles," I muttered, more to myself than to anyone else.

"Let's hope she spends more time reading our submissions than she did reading about this conference," Alissa said.

"Who knows? At least she's just as bored as the rest of us," Jetta said, laughing. I smiled.

I *loved* hearing that last part. Mari was almost never bored. Ever. She might have had fluctuating feelings about our submissions and pitches, but boredom wasn't one of them. Not that Mari would have admitted to being bored here. Oh, no. That would have required her to admit she was wrong.

As my co-workers and I walked down the halls, I enjoyed listening to them describe their best sleep-inducing instructors. The... one... who... talked... like... this... The one who almost put herself to sleep as she babbled on about the history of different font types. Another whose voice was at such a whisper that it wasn't even worth straining to hear. I think I even had one or two of those instructors that morning.

By the time we reached the makeshift food bar for the second of two fifteen-minute breaks, I was suddenly on my own. Joe and Alissa wanted to spend some private time together. Jetta got distracted by one thing or another and was nowhere to be found.

I was in desperate need of coffee. It took all the energy I had to keep my daydreams as such and not let them turn into real dreams, and I was now drained. At this point, coffee was the only thing I could think of to keep me awake.

I had never been one of those students who thrived on intellectual stimulation sans my beloved *cafeína*. I didn't have a morning cappuccino because—surprise, surprise—it took me too long getting ready to stop at the coffee shop, and my single-cup coffee maker was on the fritz again.

After several minutes of searching, I still couldn't seem to locate my desired beverage anywhere. As far as I could tell, no one around me was drinking the coveted coffee, either.

I checked my watch. Eight minutes until those unbearable classes began again.

Sighing in frustration, I turned around to see a handsome man holding out a cup of coffee to me.

Chapter Two

"Thank you." I smiled as I took the cup from the handsome man's hand.

The man smiled in return. "You're welcome."

He appeared to be about six feet tall, in his early thirties, with dark cocoa-colored hair, thin, black-rimmed glasses, a faint bronze-y complexion, and the prettiest turquoise eyes I'd ever seen. He had a perfectly trimmed beard, something I assumed was a mostly permanent feature on his face. From what I could tell through his soft gray suit, his body looked fit but not overly so, which I liked because I wasn't too keen on huge muscles.

He was so attractive, I almost wanted to touch him just to make sure he was real. Looking at him did this whole heart fluttering/body tingling/butterflies in the stomach thing to me. My biggest problem was I didn't know how to make it stop.

"How did you know I needed this?" I gestured to the cup.

He grinned. "You had pretty desperate 'coffee eyes.'"

There was no holding in a laugh at that nor was there any controlling the blush of knowledge which spread across my cheeks. I knew I'd definitely been in a coffee craze before and wasn't surprised to hear it happened again.

"I do have to warn you," he continued, "that it tastes good only with an extraordinary amount of sugar and cream. Well, relatively speaking. But then, I never drink coffee."

"So, why now?" I asked, taking a sip and realizing that he was absolutely right about the taste. While it was surprisingly strong, the coffee was so stale, I think I would have preferred a cup of thick, oily mud. The aftertaste alone was enough to make me want to throw up. The only pleasant thing about the coffee was its aroma.

He led me over to the coffee station as he answered, "I think even the peppiest of pep squad members would need the caffeine to stay awake here. I'm not sure soda will cut it."

While nodding in agreement, I stirred five individual packets of sugar and about a quarter cup of creamer into my coffee. After a tiny sip, I added one more sugar packet, then figured it was good enough to take a large chug. I wanted to limit the number of times the coffee slid over my taste buds, preferring to gulp it down at widely spaced out intervals as opposed to sipping all of it.

I took a moment to glance at the dwindling crowd in the room. Still no familiar faces. At least no one from my office was around. I watched some of the others to see who was attempting to choke down any of the inedible food. Less than a quarter of them had something other than doughnuts.

I turned to the handsome man again. He tugged at his pale gray tie a little, then took another sip of the awful beverage. Probably forcing it down the way I did with mine.

"What ad agency are you with?" I asked him. "I don't think I've seen you at any of these conferences before. And believe me, I've had to attend a lot of them."

"I'm not with an agency, actually." He gulped the rest of his coffee, cringing at the end before tossing the paper cup into a nearby garbage can. "I work for a bank. My bosses got together and decided having all their employees attend these kinds of seminars would be a good idea. This is our first one."

How *very* unfortunate for him. "Oh, I'm so sorry. Was this close to what you expected?"

"Uh, well, maybe. I didn't know what to expect."

"Yeah. I understand. It can vary depending on the effort the organizers put in."

"Not much effort here, huh?" He chuckled, and I joined in for a moment or two.

"So, why did your bosses want you all here? If you don't mind my asking."

"The top executives are on this whole 'understanding' thing. Which is great, or it was at first. It's now gotten a little out of hand. They think we should know exactly what the ad team goes through to give us what we need."

"Ah, yes," I nodded solemnly. "The plight of the copywriter. One of the more underrated plights, I believe. We seldom receive the sort of international attention we deserve."

He smiled. "How long have you been a copywriter?"

"About three or so years now, not counting my six-month internship."

"Do you like it?"

"Usually. It's a great career. There are good days and bad, of course. But when we're stuck at places like this, I absolutely hate it. This has to be one of the worst conferences ever. Although, you managed to brighten up my day." I smiled at him.

"You mean the delicious coffee did," he deadpanned.

"Oh! Yes, it's scrumptious." I laughed, and he flashed a sexy grin.

For the most part, his eyes stayed focused on me, scanning the room maybe once during our whole conversation. It was flattering to have so much interest from him, though I wasn't one who reveled in a lot of attention. With mega curly dark honey-colored tresses, deep brown eyes, and very light brown skin, I appreciated what my half Mexican/half British heritage passed down to me, I didn't need any man's eyes on me in order to feel this way.

But it was different with the man in front of me. He wasn't the same as others I'd encountered, as far as I could tell. He seemed like he was the kind of guy who truly focused on a person. Like he enjoyed making someone feel special, just by paying attention to them. He was certainly accomplishing that with me.

"Did you always want to work in this field?"

"We were fifteen when my cousin Viola started a dog-walking venture. She asked everyone she knew to spread the word but didn't receive any calls. She hung flyers around town. Simple pages with no color, no pizzazz, and also no takers, unfortunately."

The man nodded.

"Finally, she asked for my help. It was almost the end of May, and she'd hoped to start walking dogs in June. We created a new flyer together and hung them all over town. Her entire summer schedule filled up within two weeks. Every day from June to September was jam-packed with dog-walking and even pet-sitting jobs. It wasn't just because of me, obviously, but the success of our 'campaign' put a huge smile on my face for days. That solidified my decisions for college. I actually earned my degree in Communications Studies, but I took every advertising course available to me. What about you? Do you have the job you've always wanted?"

As I choked down a few more gulps of my putrid beverage, he began telling me about his education history: a year or two of college, an Associate's Degree, and *lots* of hard work. Most of the training he received was on the job, helping him quickly move up in his company. He hadn't gotten very far into his history or even to telling me what company he worked for when I noticed the room was almost empty by now. I reluctantly figured we should move on to our next seminars.

After that morning, I did not want to be late again. Well, that wasn't entirely true. I wanted to not even be there at all. I wanted to run out of that horrible place as quickly as possible. For the sake of my job, however, I thought it best to attend the seminar on time. I couldn't afford to piss off Mari. I also couldn't afford to end up jobless.

I said as much to him, to which he replied with a nod. "Yeah, you're probably right. Back to learning all about newsletters and direct mail pieces. The highlight of my life." He gave me a sweet grin. "It was very nice meeting you, Christabel."

"H-how did you—" I began before remembering my basic blue and white "Hi! My name is: *Christabel Evans*" name tag still remained on the upper left front of my chocolate brown blazer. I colored again. "Right. Well, it was very nice meeting you, too, uh—"

I noticed that while I still had my name tag on, his was gone. I got the impression that he hated wearing name tags and got rid of them as soon as he could, if he even wore the tags at all. My creative director would have said that this meant he wasn't a team player, but I simply took it as a sign that he refused to do insignificant things he didn't like purely because it was expected of him.

"Eric Griffin."

"Nice to meet you, Eric." We politely shook hands, which sent a tingling shock all through my right arm up into my shoulder. "And thanks again for the coffee." I slightly lifted my cup to him.

"My pleasure." He grinned again before walking away.

I downed the rest of my disgusting drink, throwing my cup into the trash before rushing off once more.

In my last seminar of the day, a tutorial on the various types of brochures and how to format them, I found myself near not only Jetta but also my new handsome acquaintance. Eric had grinned at me when he first walked through the door. He sat a few chairs away from me, in the closest empty seat. As I stole a glance at him, I caught him staring in return before moving his eyes. He stood and took a few steps nearer before glancing in my direction again. After a beat or two, he stepped even closer, taking a chair that had opened up as the instructor stepped to the front of the room. Eric was now just on the other side of my neighbor.

He then asked my neighbor if they could switch places so he could "see the projection screen better," which put him next to me. He was less than a foot from me in his new spot. A better viewpoint was his reason, but something inside me said there was another motive.

Everything the instructor did on the screen, we were supposed to do on the computers in front of us. Easy things like formatting the text, copying and pasting on a different page, leaving room for graphics, things like that. As far as I could tell, everyone in the room had a good view of the projection screen from where they sat.

Actually acknowledging this to myself, however, made me nervous and a little giddy. I mean, Eric wasted no time doing his best to move from a chair several feet away to one a mere five inches away. What else could have been his motive?

Once everyone was settled and the speaker began, I slyly cast a glance in Eric's direction. His eyes looked exhausted behind his glasses, and his tie, which had been straight and tidy when we first met, was loosened to the middle. His suit jacket was no longer on his body but hung on the back of the chair he was slumped in. He looked like he couldn't wait for the lecture to be over, and I didn't blame him. I felt exactly the same.

From my other side, I saw Jetta checking him out as well. Her dark eyes went up then down and back, pausing in quite a few places. She quickly nudged me in a way that Eric could not see. "Who is that?" she whispered. "He's hot!"

I was opening my mouth to answer back when my attention was diverted by the deafening voice of the instructor. His countenance became more animated as he stepped away from his own computer to talk about direct mail brochures and the various fonts he preferred using in them.

At any moment, I expected Jetta to start sliding me notes, just like in middle school. Even at age twenty-seven, she had a history of doing that during boring seminars. During interesting ones, I couldn't get a word out of her. This one kind of fell in the middle. The topic itself was a total snooze fest, but the passionate instructor was young enough to hold Jetta's attention.

Quite frequently during those ninety minutes, Eric's gaze focused on my own. Our nearness might have hindered us from watching each other so much for fear of getting caught by the other. This didn't seem to be the case, though. Maybe the first few times we were caught looking, we glanced away, but this shyness quickly disappeared. I noticed his eyes were on me more than either the projection screen or his computer. He didn't even gaze past me to ogle Jetta, which was something almost every other guy would have done. Eric's eyes stayed on me alone. And he never seemed fazed or surprised by me turning my eyes to him. In fact, he smiled at me every time.

The last time this happened, I felt a rush of tingles up and down my body and had to glance away before feeling any more. I had experienced little sparks shaking hands with him, but that was nothing compared to the energy that filled me in this moment. It was an intense, sort of heady sensation. I didn't even want to know what else would happen if I looked at him again. I couldn't. He had already attracted way too much of my attention.

I had no clue what the instructor was going on about. The few things he'd typed on the screen when I was still paying attention had been cleared off. I didn't understand the jumble of new words being projected. Finally, I forced my eyes to stay on my blank computer screen. I didn't think it was a good idea to start fantasizing about the guy sitting next to me. It felt way too much like high school already. I wasn't sure if Eric ever gave his attention back to the instructor. The bit of him I could see from the corner of my eye didn't seem to be typing anything into his computer.

At the end of the lecture, Eric stepped away, giving me a chance to breathe. Jetta had stepped away as well, most likely to find a spot to look at him some more. I was busy rearranging the various brochures, pamphlets, and study guides I had received throughout the day in my bag when, from behind me, Eric's deep voice spoke softly in my ear.

"It was nice seeing you again, Christabel. You brightened my day, too." He spoke so quietly and so close to me that I flushed at how intimate the moment was. It had sent more tingles through me than I even knew were possible to feel.

When I turned around to answer, he was already gone.

"You know him?" Jetta asked excitedly, coming around to my seat.

"His name is Eric," I told her. I continued arranging my various pamphlets, knowing full well that just about everyone else had thrown theirs away, Jetta included. "I met him earlier."

Her excitement grew to the point that I thought her eyeballs would fall out of her head from her eyes being so wide. "Details, please!" she grinned, pulling my bag away from me. "How? Where were you? What happened with you two?"

"It was during break," I answered slowly. My head was actually too full of him to give any decent details to Jetta. I wasn't even sure I wanted to give her the details. I kind of liked the idea of keeping him to myself.

"But how did it happen?" she asked again. Her face was begging me to feed her whatever information I could.

"It really wasn't a big deal." I grabbed my bag and zipped it closed.

We exited the room into the corridor, with Jetta throwing out a million questions about Eric, and met up with Joe and Alissa. Alissa was my age and a recent hire, having started four months before the conference, which was the reason she often stayed out of the "awful Mari" story swaps. Joe had been around for longer, both in life and at the agency. He was thirty and had been at Madison Advertising for nine years. He was once offered a creative director position at both a competing agency and our own but turned them down. He said he loved his current job far too much to leave it for anything else.

I couldn't fathom why. It would have meant more responsibility, though possibly slightly less actual work—or at least less creative work—but it wasn't like being a copywriter was always the easiest or best job in the world.

"Hey, Jetta! Hey, Christabel!" Alissa smiled, her arm linked inside Joe's. The medium-sized waves in Alissa's auburn hair rippled with each head turn she made glancing from Jetta to me and back again. "Long day, huh?"

"The longest Saturday of my life!" Jetta sighed, having now forgotten all about Eric.

"Joe and I are heading to the dinner they're having here. We aren't expecting a lot out of it, but they should at least have alcohol. Do you two want to join us?"

Jetta nodded intensely. "Absolutely! I'm dying for a drink. Today has been *such* a bore. Nine hours of listening to crap we've known for years. I've never had such a torturous day in my life."

"I don't think so." I shook my head in turn. I had inclination to talk with Eric again, but I assumed there was no way he would attend the dinner. And after seeing the food during break, I had no desire to view any more from this place.

"Oh, come on! There will be lots of champagne!" Alissa smiled again. "Well, extremely cheap champagne, but still. And we're taking a detour to a nearby bar before heading home. It's only two doors down from here. That way, we don't have to drive anywhere until we're ready. Plus, I hear the bar has really delicious cocktails."

"Thanks, but I just want to take off my shoes and relax."

"I'm sure you can do that, too." Joe smiled, his free hand holding a roll of what I could only imagine to be his own day's collection of pamphlets. Knowing him, they were about to have a date with a trash can. I was surprised he hadn't tossed them sooner. "I doubt anyone would notice."

"Sure, Joe. That's exactly the kind of impression I want to give those people about me. Can you imagine the stories? And worse, the exaggerations? 'You would *not* believe the stupid, drunk chick I saw last night, walking around with no shoes and only half her clothes!' Uh, no thanks."

Except I didn't actually say any of this.

What I really said was, "That's okay. You guys go on without me. I'd rather head home and forget all about being here." Well, with the exception of Eric, but I kept quiet about this little detail.

"Are you sure?" Jetta asked. She was composed on the outside, but inside, I knew she was pretty disappointed. She saw it as me turning down an opportunity to hang out with the girls. Joe was an unavailable man, and therefore didn't count in Jetta's eyes.

"Yep. Just be safe."

"All right, Mom," she laughed. "Don't worry. See you Monday?"

"See you Monday." I turned to Alissa. "Bye!" I hugged her and gave a wave to Joe before I headed for the parking lot.

Chapter Three

The oven door creaked open before the rich, slightly spicy aroma of chicken enchilada lasagna wafted out to me. I sat a room away on the red linen sofa, my eyes momentarily closed to fully enjoy the scent of my favorite meal. An Italian classic turned on its head in a totally different country? Who wouldn't love that?

"How's the project coming along?" Logan's deep voice boomed softly next to my ear.

At twenty-five, Logan had been in my life for fourteen years, but, for most of that time, not in any serious capacity. We never talked in school. The first time I remember giving him more than a half-second glance was during a class we had one semester of senior year.

When we were in school, he was just a smart, scrawny, fair yet freckled kid. Lucky for me, he turned into a smart, sexy, still freckled man. A sexy man who became one of my dearest friends, then my boyfriend.

Logan was putting his incredible culinary skills to good use. He had a special gift for cooking but stayed modest about it.

My eyes rushed open again as I answered, "Very well. Thanks."

He towered in front of me at nearly six-foot tall as he stood. His muscles were noticeable under a nice blue button-down shirt, his sleeves rolled to the elbows the way I liked. He loved to work out and did so on a daily basis.

I, meanwhile, couldn't remember the last time I had even touched my Pilates resistance band. I wasn't exactly sure I knew where it was, either. Or if I could recall what to do with it.

As Logan stood in the living room, his pale green eyes slowly took in the fact that I no longer held my notebook and pen or even my laptop but my newest issue of *People* magazine. His voice hardened ever-so-slightly. "I thought you were supposed to be working right now. That's what you told me you were doing. What happened?"

"I *am* working," I playfully rolled my eyes with a smile. I hoped the smile would hide the fact that I absolutely despised it when he asked me that question. Sometimes the same words, always the same tone. *"Why aren't you working now?"* Never a question I had an easy answer for or, more honestly, one he would like.

I was currently assigned to a print ad project for a local chain of car dealerships that was to appear in newspapers, periodicals, etc., throughout the Midwest. We were also assigned to create a commercial that was to be aired on TV stations in all the biggest cities in the area, including Chicago, Milwaukee, Green Bay, and Indianapolis.

Unfortunately, I was suffering from major mental block. I could not stare at my outline or mock layout anymore.

Hearing Logan question my work habits didn't help any. Annoying me was so not a good way to make me work more. It usually made me want to stop what I was doing altogether. Unfortunately for both of us, Logan hadn't learned that. His questioning bordered on him being, well...

I wanted to say "an ass," but I had decided a while ago to give up swearing. I was trying to stick with it, but it wasn't easy. I couldn't even believe some of the things that used to come out of my mouth.

So, I gave up swear words altogether. I even created an incentive to stay on track. Most people put money in a jar, but I wasn't married and lived by myself. It was all my money anyway.

What I decided on was so ingenious. I had these hideously ugly, ginormous, putrid green and yellow bracelets given to me by a distant relative for one birthday or another many years ago. The colors together actually looked like a mixture of baby poo and pea soup-tinged vomit. One would almost expect a smell to go along with the ugly.

For every swear word I said, I had to wear those disgusting bracelets the entire next day. There was no cheating by staying home where no one could see me. I had to go out in public with them, whether I worked that day or not.

There I was in this moment, avoiding the toxic "a" word in order to avoid the hideous bangles, wishing Logan would let me read my magazine in peace.

"I'm researching right now," I continued, "which I need to do before I write down any ideas. What if I unwittingly came up with the same idea as one in here and pitched it to the team? I'd look like an idiot."

"You seriously think you would come up with an ad for a car dealership that's the same as one in an entertainment magazine?"

"It's possible," I said with an edge to my tone.

"Whatever you say," Logan replied with a casual shrug, already working his way back to the kitchen. "If you have time for a break, dinner is almost done." He glanced over his shoulder. While I was certain he didn't believe me about the research, he never let on. That made me smile inside.

"Okay. Thank you." I grinned on the outside, too, watching the back of his dark blond head disappear through the kitchen doorway.

Then I returned to my quick page-flipping. I figured if I lingered too long on any one page, Logan would catch me and ask me the ever-dreaded question again.

The sentiment was often misunderstood. Logan wasn't a jerk or anything like that. Quite the opposite, really. Well, almost always.

We'd been together for about seven months. He had his life; I had mine. Logan and I were committed to each other but not in any deep, serious, "together forever" kind of way. I knew we didn't want to give up on each other because of a silly, little thing like not being in love. Neither of us ever mentioned wanting to stray from that. I certainly wasn't in the market for a true love, nor would I be at any time in the future that I could see. I wasn't sure I even knew how to fall in love.

Then there was Logan in all his indecisive glory.

He was in his sort-of third year of college. He took some time off during his sophomore year to "figure a few things out." He had quite a habit of taking time off in order to decide what his life should be like—a habit that continued into our relationship.

Three months after we started dating, he told me he finally knew what he wanted to do with his life. Since he was sure, he wasn't going to give up until he had it. Whatever that meant.

I was happy that he'd possibly found his future career as a graphic designer. He had a lot of talent for art and visual effects—though it was difficult at first explaining to him that, while it was greatly appreciated, I didn't need his help with my work. My company already employed graphic designers, and the last thing I wanted to do was waltz in there and tell them how I thought their jobs should be done.

His constant wavering about what he truly wanted out of life made me more than a little nervous. And he never outright said, "I don't know." It was always, "I'm positive this is the right path for me." Followed a few days later with, "No, this other path. This is exactly what I need. I'm sure of it." And so on.

This was one reason in my long list of why I was certain we'd never have a lifelong relationship. I had no desire to hear, "I'm positive I want to marry you," leading me to plan a wedding, only for him to change his mind later with, "No, I'm sure I can't. We have to call it off. Cancel everything." This would inevitably be followed in another few days or weeks by, "Wait, yes. I *will* marry you. Right now."

I mean, the toll that would take on my nerves, not to mention my sanity, was more than I could bear. I was convinced any marriage with Logan would surely lead to divorce court almost as quickly.

Like I really wanted *that* in my life. Quickie marriage, quickie divorce. Not exactly a happy ending.

No. Our relationship worked as it was. We still shared our lives together in our own ways. We made time for each other but not obsessively so. We had date nights when we could.

Knowing how much my job meant to me, Logan was always super supportive of me bringing work to our dates as long as I actually worked.

This was one of those working nights. Logan said he would make dinner while I worked if I agreed to finish soon enough to watch his favorite movie.

Obviously, I'd said yes. He'd offered me a night with my boyfriend, my favorite food, and his favorite movie.

After I flipped through the entire magazine, I made my way to the kitchen. It was a good thing dinner was done because until this point, I hadn't realized how hungry I was. The aroma that was delightful in the living room had intensified into the most delicious scent that could ever fill a room.

Logan had already gathered his eclectically mismatched plates and slightly dull silverware, placing everything on the white Formica countertop along with a handful of printed paper napkins. As I stepped closer, I noticed he'd poured one glass of red wine and was filling a second.

"Thank you." I smiled as he handed a slightly worn glass to me.

We each sipped our wine for a few moments. I watched as Logan set down his glass and grabbed a couple of pot holders to pull the casserole out of the oven. After deftly closing the oven door with a knee, he placed the lasagna on an unused burner to cool. Once he removed the oven mitts, he carried the silverware and napkins to the table, then stepped closer to me again. I took another sip of my drink, my eyes not focused on anything at this point.

All I could think about was my project. I concentrated on a few details at a time. The dealerships sold a variety of cars, all "previously owned." *Never* "used" unless someone wanted to see steam come out of the dealership's owner. They had locations throughout the city and suburbs. Most of the locations had even been in business for decades. All pretty standard stuff. From what I could tell, my client desired something completely outside the typical car ad box but not in any cheesy or annoying way.

Well, I didn't do cheesy, and I certainly didn't do annoying. This didn't make my job any easier, though.

"You okay?"

I jumped a bit at the sound of Logan's voice. "Yeah. I'm fine." I gave a small grin.

His eyes searched my face for an honest answer.

I sighed. "It's this stupid print ad. It has me so frustrated. This is a huge campaign, and we're under a lot of pressure right now. Mari has been harassing us more than usual. Her claws come out for any and every reason she can come up with. I know I'm on the brink of the *perfect* wording, but I just cannot seem to figure it out."

Logan wrapped an arm around my lower back, gently kissing the side of my head. "Anything I can do?"

I thought about his offer for a moment, absently swirling my wine around in the glass. It smelled exactly the way I imagined Italy did. Rich and robust and slightly earthy. It made me want to visit Italy. Or at least want to eat its food. Warm, hearty Italian food. Maybe a different take on Italian food?

Then I realized what I wanted.

"You can feed me." I smiled at my boyfriend.

"Are you hungry?"

"Starved."

"Well, baby, let's eat." After pulling away from each other, we dished out the food, topping the entrée with a sprinkle of cilantro and a dollop of sour cream. We carried our plates and wine glasses to the slightly faded, oak-veneered dining table located on the far end of the tiny kitchen.

Logan's apartment was small but clean and very masculine in taste: Black appliances, red, orange, and black furniture, chrome fixtures, a million video games and consoles, and a giant flat screen TV. Whenever we were at his place, he always said how comfortable he felt there. While I wondered at that sometimes—I thought the place a bit harsh and cold—it still made me happy that he at least liked his home. It was definitely a step up from the place he used to share with a few of his friends. That apartment always smelled like dirty feet, no matter what they did.

As we ate in the practically dollhouse-sized breakfast nook, Logan and I were a little quieter than normal. I couldn't exactly say why. Well, I couldn't speak for Logan. I was still preoccupied with work. The magazine had actually inspired me but not because of the advertisements. My muse was a small story I had read, completely unrelated to my project, that sparked something inside me. The gears in my brain were turning at lightning speed as I mentally divided each bit I liked into the pieces that would really work for me.

My full fork was halfway to my mouth when I quickly dropped it on the plate and jumped up from the table. I ran back to the living room as I heard Logan follow behind. I sat on the sofa in a rush and grabbed my computer off the table. Before my actions registered, I began typing frantically into the laptop. Letters, words, sentences. It all looked like a blur of black and white.

Out of the corner of my eye, I could see Logan desperately wanting to ask me what in the world was going on. He stayed silent, however. I think he was actually a little scared. He switched between crossed arms and hands on hips then back again. At one point, I think he opened his mouth, but nothing came out.

After a minute or two, my ideas safely stored, I calmly shut the computer and returned it to the coffee table. I moved my eyes up to Logan's face, only to see him giving me a very confused look.

"I got it!" I smiled.

He gave a small laugh, shaking his head. He pulled me to my feet, softly kissing my lips before walking with me hand-in-hand back to our waiting dinner.

Chapter Four

The next morning, I did a few last-minute touchups in my foyer mirror on my way out the door before hurrying to my car. While I worked in Chicago, I lived in Oak Park, which meant I had to take the expressway in. It might not have always been during the "normal" rush hour, but it sure felt like it to me. I always tried to leave extra early to allow for traffic, but I usually ended up at least a minute or two late.

This day was no different, I realized, glancing at the clock on the car's radio. I quickly parked in a nearby parking garage and walked down to the agency. It was rather warm for a late September morning, and I carried my jacket with me during the short trek.

Our agency was really reasonable on the rules of attire. We had to look presentable but could still be comfortable at the same time, meaning while we could wear jeans to the office, they couldn't have huge holes or large stain marks on them.

Unfortunately for me, on this day there were client meetings at our office. Standard business attire was required. This rule pertained to all employees whether or not they were going to be in said meetings, especially when a major account was involved. The higher-ups, as in Mari, couldn't dare risk having clients happen upon jeans and T-shirt clad copywriters. Oh, no. Too "unprofessional." A lot of my colleagues still showed up in suits with T-shirts instead of button-downs. I mean, that *was* their idea of dressed up.

I wore my favorite knee-length teal pencil skirt, with a silky coral camisole and heather gray cardigan on top. Hanging from my neck was my favorite burnt orange, oversized necklace. I held in one hand the matching jacket to the skirt, to be worn when away from my desk, and in the other, my oversized purse.

My new light gray tweed heels clicked along the concrete as I walked just outside the building that housed the advertising agency. As soon as I entered the mostly empty lobby, I said hello to Eleanor, the elderly receptionist at the entrance to the building. In all her eighty years, she had clearly enjoyed more than her fair share of ice cream sundaes. She sported plenty of faint wrinkles and short, stark white hair. She was one of the few people who had been around since Madison's very early days.

I took an elevator up to my floor, stopping to talk to Jetta on the way to my desk.

"Hey!" Jetta smiled, swigging the last few drinks of her Starbucks latte. She tipped the cup up as high as she could. I heard both coffee and air being sucked out of the opening as she savored the final drops. "How was your date last night, Chrissie?" she asked with sparkling eyes.

"It was nice." I tried to make my voice sound as bouncy as possible, but I was afraid it came out a little flat.

"Nice? That's all you can give me? Christabel, 'nice' is something you say when you have dinner with your grandparents at Thanksgiving. Not a night alone with your boyfriend. In his apartment, no less." She took a moment to look toward my desk. "Though, I don't see a huge bouquet of lilies or daffodils over there. It couldn't have been that nice."

"Well, it *was* nice."

"So maybe the flowers haven't arrived yet?" She raised her eyebrows.

Like Logan could have afforded to send me anything like that, anyway. "Jetta, no. We didn't do anything you think he would send me flowers for. It wouldn't even occur to him to send a floral arrangement after spending the night together making love."

Jetta's mouth dropped into a frown.

"Hey, Logan and I were lucky enough to have a longer evening together than we expected. My work didn't take me too long, either. I was a bit tired once I was done with it."

"Oh, I see. Too tired to do that?"

She was not going to let it go, was she? "We had a very sweet time." I adjusted the bag on my shoulder.

"Romantic?" She raised her eyebrows again.

I must not have been giving her a good enough story thus far. If it wasn't full of sex, she at least wanted it full of romance.

"Yeah, a little. He doesn't do the whole romantic thing. But it was really sweet."

She put a hand up. "Okay, enough with the gushing. Too mushy. Too sappy. You're making me jealous here."

I laughed.

"How was the rest of it?" Her voice had lost its excitement.

"Dinner was delicious as always."

"Why doesn't he just train to become a chef and be done with it?" Jetta asked while pitching her takeout cup in the garbage can under her desk. It must have been a rushed morning for her, since she usually used a refillable cup to save waste.

I heaved a sigh. "Don't know. I mean, you know him. He can't make up his mind about anything."

Her eyes stared at my left wrist. "Haven't seen those for a while. What did you do? Call Logan an inattentive ass? Because you would be right."

I tried pulling my sleeve over the SWBs, aka Swear Word Bracelets. Jetta liked calling them the Ugly-Ass Bracelets, but I couldn't or I would have ended up wearing them a heck of a lot more. "I accidentally called some stupid woman a bitch. Oops!" My hand rushed to my mouth.

Jetta laughed. "Guess you're wearing them tomorrow, too."

"Guess so," I sighed. "I need to get to my desk to make some notes. I had a great idea for our project that came to me during the drive here. It's expanding on the idea I came up with during dinner last night. I want to be organized before our morning meeting."

"Okay." She smiled, turning to her own computer.

At our agency, the copywriters were divided into three main creative teams, three on each. The teams were divided even more when needed, which happened quite a lot. Sometimes, more of us were on a team, such as for a bigger campaign. All teams had their own graphic designer but shared the same creative and art directors. Jetta and I were in the same group—the only team with two female copywriters.

From the beginning of my employment at Madison, I was almost always on Jetta's team. Though I didn't know management's reasoning for this, I liked to think it was because we worked so well together.

Shortly after I finished my notes, Jetta and I headed downstairs. Our meeting was with Mari and Paolo, one of our account executives. He was not technically a part of our creative team, but he was the one that dealt with the clients the most. Paolo was the liaison between the client and us. We were to present to him our concepts for the current campaign and wait for feedback.

I had already exchanged my sweater for my jacket, and Jetta quickly put on her deep scarlet blazer, simultaneously admiring my forty-percent off Nordstrom score. I, in turn, glanced down at her shoes and smiled.

She was about five feet tall and liked to wear heels just as high. She also had incredibly good taste when it came to shoes. When it came to style, in general. Jetta knew how to balance work-appropriate and fashion-forward. I guessed she made a good career choice. Her daring ensembles wouldn't have worked as well in less creative fields.

While riding the elevator downstairs, I asked Jetta what she did with the rest of her weekend.

"Well, the dinner after the conference was pretty lame. The bar didn't have any good music playing, either. I danced with this hot guy for a while, but his girlfriend—the one he didn't tell me about—showed up so I went home early."

"Early being…?"

"About midnight."

"Right." I smiled. Pretty early considering I left them at six or so.

"How do I look?" Jetta asked quickly.

Thus began our meeting ritual.

It all started two years before because of an attractive man on our client's team. Jetta wanted him from the moment she saw him—despite the fact that agency employees were strictly forbidden to date clients. I was required to inform her of any flaws that needed fixing before every meeting with this particular man, a top executive in his department.

I glanced at Jetta. "Like Picasso painted that dress on you."

She looked down and smiled. "Yeah, it's pretty fierce, huh? I love the midi length on this one. The other dress I considered was too short."

The elevator stopped at the conference room floor, and we joined the other copywriter from our team in the corridor. As we walked to the correct room, another creative team and their client stepped out of the meeting space next door. To my surprise, Eric happened to be among them.

Chapter Five

I couldn't even begin to express how shocked I was. *Eric*. In *my* building. Flesh and bone and heartbreakingly good looks.

It could not have actually happened. I was just seeing things. I mean, surely he'd have told me his company had hired my agency. He'd have no reason not to. Then I remembered that we'd never gotten around to what companies we worked for.

I blinked to refocus my eyes. He turned his head and glanced at the elevators. In doing so, we caught each other's gaze. A wide smile broke out on his face. Eric said something to his associate then strolled over to me.

"Hey, Christabel." His bright expression looked even happier up close.

And he remembered my name.

My heart sped up at the sound of it.

"Hey, Eric. I'm surprised to see you here."

"Same." But he didn't appear weirded out by it.

"Griff?" The man he'd been talking to was suddenly next to us. "We have to go."

"Maybe I'll see you soon," Eric told me. He grinned again.

Then he was gone, into the elevator nearby.

Jetta returned to me from wherever she'd disappeared. "Who was that? Are you okay?" she whisper-asked, physically ushering me through the doorway.

I realized I'd been blocking the entrance when Paolo and Natalia, one of our graphic designers, quickly shuffled in after us. Our other team member also entered the room, as did an intern and Mari's assistant. Mari was right behind them, leaving me no time to explain anything to Jetta.

We sat around the large, rectangular black oak table. Several stacks of notes were in front of us all, as were a few physical props, laptops for video demonstrations, and large-sized mock-ups. As soon as we were settled, I heard Mari's voice ask for volunteers to share their concepts. A colleague shared their thoughts first. I couldn't tell exactly who it was. I wasn't paying attention. It could have been Jetta, for all I knew.

I'd completely forgotten about my own ideas, the ones I'd typed and was absently folding the corners of, until Jetta nudged me and asked if I wanted to discuss them with the team.

I didn't have an answer.

Mari cleared her throat as an indication of annoyance.

It took a full ten seconds of me staring blankly at Jetta for me to have any clue as to what she was talking about. She gave me an earnest "say something or you will lose your job!"

look while at the same time appearing as nonchalant as possible to everyone else.

"Your ideas?" Mari prompted tersely.

I looked back at Jetta again before it clicked. "Oh! Oh, yes. Yes, I have some ideas I came up with."

I could hardly even remember the words that flew out of my mouth. All I could say was that my best concept, the one I worked on while at Logan's, was generally well-liked. I had the floor for only a few minutes before they moved on to someone new.

Three agonizing hours later, our meeting was over, and everyone slowly headed out of the conference room. Time to return to our desks and begin the grueling task of trying to please Mari with more brilliant changes to already brilliant ideas. We were used to road construction in Chicago, but getting this kind of detour in our jobs really, *really* sucked.

While most of the others took the stairs, Jetta and I walked to the elevators once again.

Eric was long gone by this point, and even if he wasn't, I didn't know if I could form enough words to talk to him again. I was still in a state of utter shock. How was it possible that life had thrown us together like this?

Once the others in the elevator got off on their floor and no one else was within earshot, Jetta asked, "Okay, what is going on with you? What happened in there?"

I knew I couldn't keep it to myself. "Do you remember the cute guy we saw at the seminar the other day?"

"Which one?" she laughed, her eyes sparkling again.

She'd met a lot of men that Saturday, so describing Eric to her and placing him in her mind was going to be a little tricky. I gave her the best description I could, emphasizing his gorgeous eyes, to no avail. "You have to remember him. It was our last workshop of the day. He sat next to me, and you were on my other side. He talked to me before he left."

"Oh, right! Ethan or Derek or something. Yeah, he was tantalizingly sexy. What about him?" She pushed the button for our floor again since the elevator had passed our stop. A few unknown people from the higher floor joined us.

"Eric. And he was here."

Jetta's light brown eyes grew wide. "He came here to see you?" she whispered the best she could despite her excited curiosity. "When? How did I miss that? Did you talk to him?"

"We said hi. Not much else. He didn't come here to see me. I had no idea he would even be here. He was in the meeting with Joe's team."

"Oh, he must be with their new client. I heard someone talking about that last week. I guess our agency is being hired to completely overhaul their bank's image as soon as possible."

"Why so fast?"

"Their executives want people to know that their bank has become an even better company that truly cares about not only its employees and clients but all consumers. That the bank's bosses understand the problems people have had. That they haven't been ignored all these years. Something along those lines."

I immediately knew what this meant. We had redeveloped a company's image before, and the whole process from start to finish took many months' time. Like months turning into years kind of time. The chances of my seeing Eric again had just greatly increased.

"Eric mentioned his bosses' newfound empathy for everyone and everything." We were in our general office area again, having just stepped out of the elevator.

Jetta turned to me with a curious look. "I'm assuming this guy had a lot to do with your brain lapse at the meeting."

I gave a small nod. Honestly, I hated even admitting that much. I wasn't so sure I wanted Jetta to know how much Eric affected me.

"But what about Logan?"

"What about him? And how did we go off-topic?"

She gave me a half-smile with a certain expression in her eyes. "We didn't."

I let out a short laugh.

As ridiculous as it seemed, though, I knew she was serious.

But she was completely off-base. Absolutely, entirely wrong, wrong, *wrong*. "Jetta, I'm happy with Logan. I don't need more than that."

"Okay." She stared at me, clearly waiting for more.

She knew me too well. "I hardly even know Eric. I admit that he's cute, and seeing him today definitely flustered me, but I have no interest in him. I would never look at him as anything more than a friend." A very hot friend, but still. "With or without Logan."

"If you say so." She paused. "So you wouldn't mind introducing me to Eric, right?"

I instantly felt a tightening in my chest. My mouth began to dry out. I couldn't swallow; I couldn't breathe.

"That's what I thought," Jetta sighed in singsong before sitting at her desk.

I slowly walked to my own desk, sat in my black office chair, and set my papers off to one side. I was busy pulling up a program on the computer when my cell phone rang.

"Hey, gorgeous!"

"Logan! Hey. What's up?" I asked, looking around to make sure no executives were in the area. We didn't usually get in trouble for taking personal phone calls, but I didn't want to risk anything. I never knew when a superior was going to have a problem with employees spending company hours on personal time, most especially Mari. I'd never forgive myself for jeopardizing or possibly losing my job over a stupid phone call.

"Actually, I found out that I can't come over tonight."

"Seriously?" I sighed, disappointment oozing out of me despite my best effort to keep it in.

I'd had the night planned out perfectly. As a continuation of the previous night, and also as a sort of thank you for him being so wonderful lately, we were going to have a movie night at my place. I was going to cook Logan's favorite meal of homemade macaroni and cheese, a dish he taught me—one I made only for him.

After what would probably be a late dinner, we were going to sit on my big, comfy sofa and watch my favorite movie. Nothing too cutesy or girly or anything like that. I knew what my choices were as far as holding Logan's interest for long periods of time.

"Yeah. Can't be helped."

"Um, okay. Well, what are you busy with?"

"Oh, you know. Just stuff I have to do. I'll make it up to you, though. I promise."

"I'm sure you will. I'm just bummed."

"Well, I know something that will cheer you up."

"What's that?" I thought I saw movement at Mari's door, so I tried to duck my head down behind my computer screen.

"David and Loretta are having a party this Friday."

"What for?" I looked over at the CD's office again. *Whew!* False alarm.

Logan's voice brought my attention back to my phone. I switched the phone from my left ear to my right in time to hear him say, "It's the start of their baseball playoff parties. They do it every year. You should already know that. They're your friends, too."

I did actually know that. How I'd forgotten about the party, I had no idea. I was in a dilemma, however. The prospect of a party did not actually make me feel any better. On the other hand, I knew it was something that Logan was probably looking forward to.

I suddenly found myself expressing more enthusiasm than I honestly felt. "Oh, that's right! Well, it sounds great. Lots of fun. I can't wait! So looking forward to it!"

Wow. I couldn't believe how fake I sounded. Of course, it was believable enough to pass the "Logan test."

"I know! I'm excited. I can't wait to go, either. It will be so much more fun watching the game with everyone else."

Earlier in our relationship, our date nights consisted of baseball games instead of movies. I'd finally managed to get him to cut back a little, but usually, we would simply plan dates outside of game time.

I used to be a huge Cubs fan. My adoration started when I was a kid, like Logan. I watched the games, I had the jerseys, and I knew all the players' names and stats by heart. I cheered every Cub hit and booed every bad call. This lasted for years, even into adulthood.

I just couldn't take it anymore. Losing, losing, some incredible winning, then the heartbreak of losing yet again. It became really depressing cheering on a team who didn't seem to care all that much about the game while at the same time remembering how much heart and soul they used to play with. It came to a point that I truly believed they would be perfectly fine never winning a Series again or even okay with finishing every season under .500.

That's when I gave up. I figured since they already had, what difference would it make if I did, too? Of course, I was overjoyed when they finally won the World Series. It was everything I'd ever wanted to see from the team. Unlike others, though, I couldn't say for certain when or if they might win again.

This sort of "doom and gloom attitude," as Logan called it many times, never rubbed off on him.

"That leads me to another thing," he continued, interrupting my thoughts. "I won't get to see you before the party."

"Um, okay," I said again.

I couldn't tell if I'd masked my annoyance. Not only was he postponing our date, he was also compounding the suckiness of the day. It was only Monday. Was it really necessary to go so long until our makeup date? Unfortunately, that was Logan. He was *the* embodiment of mystery and confusion when he wanted to be.

"I'm busy with a lot of things right now."

"It's okay. I understand. I probably have to work late, anyway," I added, not knowing if Mari would make us stay over or not but wanting Logan to know I'd be busy with something else, too. Why let him think I'd be sitting at home all night hoping he'd call? I had better things to do. Even if that might not be the case, I at least pretended it was.

"I have to go now, but I'll call you later. All right?" Despite having disappointed me, he voice was still cheerful.

"Yep." I turned my phone off, tossing it a little too hard into my purse before letting out yet another sigh.

Why couldn't I be as happy and carefree as Logan was?

Chapter Six

Two days later, Jetta and I were drinking coffee at her desk during our rather shortened late afternoon lunch break. As we sat, she looked around her work area and sighed. It was the kind of sigh that demanded attention.

"What's wrong?" I asked compliantly.

She sighed again. "I think I need a new office motif."

I looked around the large room, able to see all the copywriters' desks in the same area. "I wouldn't exactly call this an office." I sipped the last of my cappuccino, letting the sweet liquid linger on my tongue for a few moments before swallowing.

"You know what I mean. I'm bored with everything here." She motioned around.

Her flashy, mod desk almost made me cringe when I thought about how disorganized and mismatched my own office area was. My desk and chair matched everyone else's but not much on the desk itself matched anything.

"It's all been the same for the past four months." Jetta looked with disdain at everything near her. "The same pictures, the same ugly red clock—"

"You love that clock. Besides, there isn't much you can change, anyway."

Jetta wasn't listening, though. She was thinking. "Ooh! I've got it. Morocco!" She instantly pulled out her tablet from an immaculately organized drawer. "I've always wanted to go there, and I saw an article the other day of how to 'Create your Moroccan Dream' for under, like, five hundred bucks or something."

My mouth dropped open. "Jetta, you aren't actually going to spend five hundred dollars on your work desk, are you?"

"Of course not." She gave a dismissive wave of the hand. Then she lay the tablet on the desktop in front of us, pulled up an online catalog, and began to flip through its contents. Every few pages, she'd mark an item or two and ask me if I thought it would match an existing piece. She had a pretty good rhythm going, too, between the catalog and her latte. Flip, sip. Flip, sip.

I'd avoided the topics of both Eric and Logan up to this point but wasn't sure how long that could last. We had already covered a lot of other ground, and the redecorating sprint would only last so long.

"Any plans this weekend?" I asked, hoping to stay away from discussing the men in my life. Men. Plural. That had never, ever happened before.

"Other than our Saturday meeting?"

"Ugh. I forgot."

As imperative as this upcoming meeting honestly was, I still wasn't looking forward to it.

"You're going shopping with your sister, right?"

"Of course." Jetta grinned.

Jetta bought new furniture pieces a lot because it meant that she "needed" her sexy neighbor to help her put everything together. What she'd never told him was that she owned a set of tools and didn't actually require his help. I almost wished he was my neighbor, as I couldn't assemble furniture or fix water leaks to save my life.

I waited a moment then asked, "You still haven't dated Carlos yet because...?"

She shrugged. "Neighbor Guy has a new girlfriend. I know you are so heartbroken for me." She drew out the word "so" for dramatic effect.

"Carlos is a serial monogamist with playboy tendencies. You should steer clear of him."

Jetta ignored this. "Other than shopping and our meeting, I'm joining Joe and Alissa on a double date Saturday night."

"A double date? Won't that be awkward?"

"Just because Joe and I dated for a few weeks doesn't mean that we can't be friends now."

"I know this. But still. A date all together?"

I was the only one under forty at work that never went out with Joe, not that he didn't try. We had plenty in common, including both of us being grandchildren of immigrants. He loved hearing stories of how hard my mom's parents worked to leave Mexico and start a new life near Chicago. I felt the same about his maternal family from Greece. But Joe simply wasn't someone I envisioned myself dating. He was good enough to not take that kind of rejection personally. It was this goodness that made me consider him an attractive friend and not an attractive but kind of slutty jerk.

"It isn't a big deal." Jetta shrugged. "Alissa's setting me up with a guy her sister works with."

"What does he do?"

"He's a sportswriter," she answered, circling about five items on one page, including a bejeweled frame.

"That sounds promising." According to my standards. As long as the guy was a good person, I didn't care what he did for a living. Jetta was much pickier.

"Yeah. I guess. He's not actually into normal sports, though."

"Normal sports?" As I crinkled my eyebrows, my phone trilled. I tried not to be too excited as I pulled it out. A text from my sister. Not Logan. I shoved it back in my jacket without reading or responding.

"You know: baseball, basketball, football. Maybe soccer. He likes fly-fishing and hiking. I think he even likes rowing. Total outdoorsy type."

My phone chirped from my pocket a second time. I quickly removed it again, hoping it was finally a reply text from Logan. No such luck. I placed the phone on Jetta's desk without reading the text from a friend.

"Logan?" Jetta asked with raised eyebrows.

I shook my head.

Jetta laughed. "At this point, a date's a date."

I couldn't help but smile. "I suppose that's true. May I ask what exactly it is they think you'll like about him?"

"Well, he's single, decent-looking, well-employed, and has a pulse. What else does a guy need?"

Ridiculous as it was, this elicited another grin. I didn't know what else to say, though. Trouble was, I was too preoccupied to ask her anything else. We fell into silence. My eyes kept looking over at my phone. I tried willing it to ring, but nothing happened.

I knew Jetta had noticed something different about me because I'd noticed it, too. I was quieter than usual. I was also having difficulty giving my full attention to any one thing. There were too many thoughts inside me. Things I was having trouble understanding, like Logan and his intentions, or rather, his inattentions. And why was it that Eric was suddenly thrown into my life? Was it okay for me to want to see him again?

All my effort pretending that I wasn't distracted was a waste, yet I couldn't seem to stop.

My mom always said I wasn't very good at hiding my true feelings from loved ones because I had such a good heart. But she was my mom. She was supposed to say things like that. She once told me I never lied as a child because whenever I started to, I would cry from the knowledge that lying was hurtful to others. I honestly found that super difficult to believe.

My phone chirped once more, and I grabbed at it faster than I wanted to. It was an incoming call from my mom of all people. I sent the call to voice mail and texted her in reply.

Me: Hi Mom! At work. Call you tonight.

While I had my phone in hand, I sent a quick text to Logan asking him to call me. But would he?

My mom was always good for extra doses of support, but sometimes, she wasn't much actual help. I knew if I told her about what was going on with Logan and me, she would follow her typical advice path. She'd worry and say that I didn't need to go through something like that. That it was awful I was so upset about it. For the most part, though, she would be at a loss for answers, or answers I could use.

I probably got that from her because I was at a loss, too.

"So, how have things been with you?" Jetta asked, startling me in the quiet. Her tone was casual, but her face told me she was worried. So did the fact that she began to twist her hair straightened hair. She never did that unless she was trying to prove to me how not worried she was about something. The fact that she was willing to risk ruining her perfectly coifed hairstyle meant a lot to me, but I just still couldn't tell her.

"There's this art exhibit I was planning on attending Saturday. I might have to pick a different day now, though."

"Maybe. Who knows how long our meeting will last?"

"*Please.* If Mari has her way, we won't even dream of leaving the building until at least eight hours of intense strategizing have passed. I'm so tired of these meetings. I'm tired of the way things are with Mari in charge. I realize revisions are a part of the job, as are long periods of waiting to hear back from the clients, but it seems out of control now. Georgina would always stand up for us and end contracts if the clients wouldn't stop jerking us around."

"I guess we'll have to wait and see how it goes. Chrissie, if you hate it here so much, why don't you finally quit?"

"I can't afford to, and you know that. Besides, aren't you and I supposed to be the best here? Why would I leave?"

Jetta shrugged as she flipped another page. Because the catalog remained open in front of her, I really hoped the promise of new décor would distract her just a little longer. "Mari sucks. I know this. We all do. We all hate her. She's made our lives hell since she started. But what else is going on?"

"What do you mean?" I asked innocently.

"*Chrissie.*" She stared at me, head tilted, eyes narrowed. It was the sort of expression that meant I was totally busted.

I sighed. "Okay. Fine." I quickly filled her in on my conversation with Logan, hitting all the important stuff. "I didn't realize that when he said we wouldn't see each other until the party, he meant it."

"We've been slammed here, anyway, Chrissie. I don't think we've left the office before ten since Monday."

"Yeah, I know," I nodded. "I also didn't realize it meant we wouldn't talk, either, especially since he promised to call me."

Jetta's eyes strayed to the catalog once more before settling on me. "Yes, but he said he would do that later. 'Later' could mean in an hour, a day, or a week. It isn't very specific."

She already knew that Logan wasn't very specific in general, having used it against me in a debate on whether I should dump him. A few times, actually. "You would think he'd at least want to talk to me since he had to cancel our date."

"You have a phone. You're allowed to call him first."

I ignored this.

Jetta grabbed my phone off the desk, then put it back down with a flash of thought in her eyes. She dug out her own phone from a drawer, pressed the screen a few times, and put it on the desk in front of her. She had it on speaker, so I could hear the ringing on the other end of the line.

"Hello?" Logan's voice came through.

I nearly fell out of my chair. He answered! He freaking answered.

Jetta looked as shocked and pissed off as I felt. "Hey, Logan," she said, calm and composed. "I was wondering if you happened to get that number from your friend at work for me yet."

I crinkled my eyebrows at her in confusion, but she silently waved me off.

"I didn't know you wanted his number. Christabel didn't mention it."

"Oh!" Jetta put on an affected, "silly me" tone. "I might not have told her, now that you mention it. But would you mind? You can text me later today if possible."

"Sure. No problem," my boyfriend told her.

"Great. Thanks." Jetta hit "End Call" and looked at me with fire in her eyes. "So, his phone still works, and he has it with him."

I nodded. I looked at my own phone. Nothing from him.

What. The. Hell.

"Is there any chance of him, like, dating other women behind your back? Because he clearly has a way to answer your messages and is choosing not to. Maybe he's somewhere he shouldn't be."

I could only shake my head. I was still too livid to form words. My heart thumped in my throat, making it difficult to breathe.

Jetta held her latte at her lips for a moment then placed the cup on her desk. "Chrissie, I have to ask: Is Logan doing this again?"

"Doing what?"

"Don't do that. Don't act like you don't understand. You know what I mean. The not calling for days. The canceling of dates. Answering anyone else's calls but yours. I thought he was done with all that crap. He isn't the same kind, thoughtful guy he was in the beginning of your relationship. You and I both know this."

I didn't answer right away.

Somehow, I felt the need to defend Logan. I wanted to show Jetta and myself that he wasn't a bad guy. I wanted to prove that he wasn't as thoughtless as the circumstances were making him out to be.

In order to do so, I searched my brain for a lack of instances of such unkind, uncaring, or indifferent treatment.

Part of me knew better, though.

I never heard from Logan the entire week before my birthday in June. All my calls and messages to him went unanswered, probably even unnoticed for all I knew. He did send me a rather large bouquet of red, blue, and white roses on my actual birthday didn't deliver them in person like I'd hoped he would.

I didn't even talk to him until the day after my birthday when he could only explain his disappearance as something he couldn't control. Whether it had to do with work, family, or robbing a Vegas casino, I'll never know.

This nonchalant attitude of his was the total opposite of what I did for his birthday in July. It wasn't an extravaganza, but it did include a small party the previous weekend, a large birthday cake made by me, and a romantic dinner also made by me on the actual day. I put a lot of thought into his birthday surprises, not to mention passion. Every detail was debated over in order for thins to be precisely the way he would like it. I never considered it more than he deserved.

There had been other instances of his lack of thoughtfulness. Numerous canceled dates. Phone calls that didn't take place until a day or two or four later. One day in August, he promised to call me after waking up the next morning so we could share a cozy brunch before he had to leave town for a few days. When he neither called nor showed up, I tried my best to get in touch with him, to no avail. I didn't have any luck finding out anything for the next two terrifying days.

After eventually talking to his sister, I knew Logan was all right. She didn't give me many details, however. I had no idea where he was until he finally answered his phone halfway through his disappearance. As it turned out, Logan's friends were so excited about their planned trip to Florida for a Cubs game that they convinced him to leave a day early. He said he forgot to call me.

When we were just friends, we called, texted, and saw each other all the time. The fact that this closeness had dwindled down to its lowest point ever from March to September panicked me.

I *had* to remember something good.

Logan did buy tickets for me to see *Wicked*. He even went with me and didn't complain once, despite the fact that he'd never liked musicals. There was also the time in April when I was sick with strep throat for nearly three weeks. Logan picked up all the prescriptions for me and even brought over a large lidded container of homemade chicken noodle soup.

I finally looked at Jetta and said, "I don't know if I would call it a habit of his."

"Are you sure—I mean absolutely positive—he isn't out there sleeping around or something? You don't think that's a possibility? Seriously. Because maybe he can't handle a strong woman like you."

"Logan wouldn't sleep with someone else."

"You don't know that. I mean, I like the guy—"

I scoffed at this.

"—but who knows what he's doing without you? Do you?"

"Jetta, I trust him. I don't have to know specifics." Though they would be nice.

I saw her roll her eyes. "You can't pretend it doesn't bother you, Chrissie. He's had plenty of time to get back to you and hasn't. Why don't you just tell him how you feel?"

"I can't."

"Why not? Logan isn't a mind reader. How is he supposed to know if you don't tell him?"

"I'm not sure how I feel. Not exactly. Yeah, I'm pissed now, but... I mean, he is a great boyfriend when he wants to be."

Jetta stopped sipping her latte to catch my eyes, a serious expression in her own. "And when he doesn't?"

I had no answer for her. I had no answer for either of us.

Chapter Seven

As we entered Loretta and David's house that Friday, Logan and I were greeted by dozens of red, white and green streamers and similarly-colored pennant banners strung along the walls and door. Red and green pompom balls mingled with foam baseballs at the top corners of every wall. These were every year's party colors, no matter who was in the playoffs. Red and white stood for the ball and green for the grass since, according to David, that was all one needed to play. Minus the bat, of course, but I stopped mentioning that to him after her last over-the-top annoyance about it.

When we stepped farther into the living room, I saw a giant inflatable baseball nestled inside David's mitt-shaped beanbag chair. My eyes were attacked with everything baseball-related almost everywhere I looked. It was like being bombarded by flashing lights at a carnival.

Not only were there themed decorations jumping out from every crevice, but Logan was already leaving my side in order to join a few others in front of the TV.

I had been running a little behind that night after being smothered by revisions at work. The only reason I got out at a decent time was because I begged Jetta to cover for me, promising a favor in return. Absolutely any favor she wanted, as long as I could leave work and not disappoint my boyfriend.

Logan, however, didn't seem to appreciate my effort. He sent text after text while I was in my apartment. Well, it had started before I was through my door.

Logan: OMW

Logan: Pulling up 2 ur building.

Logan: Parked & waiting

Me: Changing now. Be out soon.

Logan: Waiting...

Logan: Waiting...

Logan: Still waiting...

He sent two more texts as I brushed my teeth, and eventually started calling as I was locking my door on the way out. When he called once more before I exited the building, I wished I could have removed the battery to speed up the process of turning the phone off.

David and Logan's friend Jesse sent quick hellos and smiles my way before immediately turning back to the on-air personalities. I walked through the large living room, across the hallway, and into the spacious kitchen. Baseball decorations overflowed in there as well.

Most everyone in the room was gathered around the island, where I proceeded to join them. I was amazed at the food choices displayed in front of me. In addition to their typical sports party fare of roast beef sandwiches, hot wings, hamburgers, and hot dogs, there was a plethora of additional food that could feed another twenty people, if not more.

I told Loretta what an awesome hostess she was.

"Oh, thank you." She smiled while opening a bottle of Zinfandel. "I had to dig through a lot of storage bins to figure out where David and I put everything because we have so much stuff now. And I was lucky to have found that table cover on sale. The one from last year was stained to the point that I just could not get it clean."

Ah, yes. The infamous juice incident. A child of someone's friend decided to open her grape juice box directly over Loretta's pristine white-and-red striped tablecloth. It didn't take much imagination to know what happened next. Purple splotches *everywhere*. Loretta, ever the gracious hostess, said it was her fault for using white fabric with kids around. Honestly, though, we all knew she was pissed.

I was surprised Loretta mentioned it. I also couldn't help but notice that family was not invited to this particular party.

Stephanie—Loretta's younger sister and my former college roommate—laughed and playfully rolled her eyes. "I'll bet you guys dream about these parties for months beforehand, don't you?"

Loretta smiled again. "Not months. Weeks maybe."

The conversation turned to Loretta and David's upcoming trip to New York City.

A few weeks before the party, David had surprised Loretta with "just because" flowers, where the plane tickets were hidden. I thought it was the cutest way to surprise someone with a vacation. And after I heard the story, I stupidly hoped Logan had that kind of surprise planned for me, too. I *loved* surprises. I loved the mystery of what a gift might be, and I loved picturing all the possibilities, like treasure hunts that lead to the gift or notes, and texts counting down the days.

Loretta was in the middle of describing the deal she got on Broadway tickets when I heard muffled voices emanating from the living room. That wasn't a big deal until I realized I recognized one of those voices. It had never fit into my world like this. My heart thumped harder as the group moved my way. I tried to extract that mystery voice from all others entering my ears, and as difficult as that was, I knew I wasn't imagining things.

Certain I was right, I turned to my left to see David entering the kitchen with Eric.

Eric looked as startled to see me as I felt to see him. My work. My friends' house. Where would I meet him next?

David began introducing Eric to everyone. When they eventually got to me, Eric smiled that smile I already adored. "Actually, Christabel and I already met."

Everyone looked surprised at this. If Logan had been in the kitchen with us, I knew he would have been shocked, too. He just would have hidden his surprise better than everyone else.

"You've met?" Loretta asked, looking back and forth between us.

I knew she was imagining all the ways I could have come in contact with Eric. All the possible random places where he and I could have found each other. Out of the corner of my eye, I saw that Stephanie also watched us. The room was much quieter. Everyone had morphed into one silent, nosy background of non-moving people.

"When was this?" Loretta continued to move her eyes from me to Eric and back again.

Eric held his smile, and his eyes were focused on me.

My caffeine addiction was well known among my friends. They would have completely understood Eric helping me with a fix. But for some reason, I knew he would keep our coffee story just between us. It was, after all, the same thing I had done.

"It was a work function last Saturday," he finally told them, quelling any further anticipation from our silent audience. "We didn't get to talk much. Unfortunately for me." His eyes moved to me again, and I grinned with a soft blush. At that moment, I was glad Logan was obsessively glued to the TV screen.

Once everyone else returned to their previous conversations or began new ones, Eric quietly sidled up to me. He wore slightly relaxed jeans and a basic white T-shirt under a toffee-colored suede jacket. He also smelled even better than the smorgasbord of delectables in front of us.

"Hi." This was accompanied by a lot more giddiness and nervousness than I wanted to show—which was none. I was trying my best to appear calm on the outside. Why in the world was that so hard to do?

"Hey," he grinned. He glanced at the food but didn't pick up anything.

I took a few calming breaths while scoping out the food as well. "So, how is it that you're here?" I couldn't help but ask.

He thought for a moment. "Well, I figured it would take too long to walk the thirty miles so I drove."

"You know what I mean," I giggled. Yes, I was a grown woman giggling like a school girl in front of a very cute boy.

In the same situation, Alissa would have brashly hidden any insecurity. Jetta would not have been fazed at all. She would have started rubbing Eric's arm or maybe even his leg. But I *giggled*.

"How are you at this party? How do you know David?" I continued.

"He and I work together. Well, at the same company, just different departments."

I couldn't believe that never occurred to me before. I had talked to David a few times about his job at Chalmers Bank. The bank with the same name as Eric's company. For whatever reason, my mind had kept this little gem of info tucked away from my memory. Thank you, brain, for spacing out exactly when I needed you.

"I knew you both worked at Chalmers, but I didn't realize you actually work *together*." This connected Eric to me in more ways than I could have imagined.

"Yeah. We've been friends for a while now."

I nodded. Then I decided to brave a subject I really wanted to talk about. "It was really nice to see you at my office on Monday."

There was something unreadable in Eric's eyes as he smiled. "It was great to see you, too. I'm sorry I had to take off. I wish we could've talked longer."

My mouth was so dry, I couldn't speak. I could only nod with a stupid, fan-girling grin.

"I was there yesterday, too," Eric said.

I wished I'd known that information sooner.

Suddenly, the remaining party guests flooded the kitchen in search of food. Loretta had taken the burgers and hot dogs off the grill and laid out platters of them on the empty counter space. I wouldn't say that Eric distracted me, but how else would I have missed a huge platter of food being set next to me?

I realized it was the second-to-last commercial break before the first pitch, the typical time for everyone to load their baseball- and mitt-designed plates and return to the TV. It was also the only time Logan stepped away from the television during a game. Any game. He was always so afraid to miss something that might not be played during highlights.

We all chose the food we wanted, only a few of the women staying behind as the rest of us headed into the living room. In addition to the rather large sofa and the glove-shaped chair, seating options included two plush reclining chairs, a few ladder-back chairs brought in from the dining room, and several oversized floor pillows for sitting wherever one wanted.

Logan immediately returned to his place on the sofa, where I snugly joined him, not really by choice. We ate mostly in silence, only the others and the people on the screen having any sort of discussions. It was our second mostly wordless dinner in less than a week, but not out of the ordinary for us. Well, maybe it was, but it certainly wasn't the first time this occurred. I assumed it also wouldn't be the last. That was just how relationships worked sometimes—or so I convinced myself.

Once the game officially began, Logan never glanced at me. I hadn't expected much, but I did naïvely hope for at least that. His eyes went from the TV to his food and back again. No looks at me; no looks at anyone else. I endured this for a little while. I had no idea why.

Silently, I scrolled through all our old texts, wanting the feelings of back then to wash over me.

Logan: Miss u so much.

Logan: Can I see u tonite? Waiting til tomorrow is too long…

Logan: Date plz. Need to see ur face.

All these and so many more, full of hope, yearning, and affection. Days when we shared laughs over the simplest, silliest things. Nights when he couldn't wait for us to both get off work, even if we had no money and no plans. We'd taken many short trips together over the spring and part of the summer, alone and with groups of our friends.

It wasn't often that he made me feel as neglected as I did the previous month or so. Not that I told him about it. Committed but not serious. If he had to stick to the agreement, so did I.

After we finished eating, Logan handed his mustard-smeared plate to me. He didn't even ask me to take it. He handed it over wordlessly. I piled our two plates together, stood up from the sofa, and had started walking out of the living room when Eric stopped me. He was standing as well, holding an empty hand out to me.

"I can take that for you," he said while looking into my eyes.

That surprised me so much that I didn't know what to say. "It's okay. You don't have to. I can do it."

"I want to," he replied, taking the dishes from my hands into his own. Our fingertips touched with a zing, causing my breath to catch.

After clearing my throat and waiting for a calm to come over me, I raised my voice enough for Logan to hear me. "Thank you for taking our empty plates into the kitchen." I hoped maybe Logan would say, "Thanks, man" or something to Eric.

He didn't.

I stood in the same spot after Eric walked away. I hadn't moved by the time he came back. He smiled at me, then looked at Logan before returning to his seat.

My body temperature had risen when Eric looked at me, to the point that I began to perspire. I needed to stop this. Like, *needed*.

After sitting next to Logan again, I took a deep breath. To catch his interest, even for a moment, I leaned into him and said, "I'm a little chilly. Do you mind if I sit closer to you?" Not that it was possible to be much closer, but I thought it a good excuse to break the silence.

He gave no reply. His eyes didn't even dart my way. It wasn't until the next commercial break, about four minutes later, when he turned to me. "Christabel, you know this is the only time I can talk to you during the game."

Other people talking during the game didn't bother Logan, but heaven forbid I decided to say anything outside the commercial breaks. No matter what I was trying to tell him. I supposed if I had to let him know my hair, or even his precious hair, was on fire, he would have ignored me.

He'd once explained to me that he simply didn't feel right asking others to stay quiet, but as his girlfriend, *I* was supposed to know better.

Under the pretense of adjusting my olive cashmere cardigan, I looked away to roll my eyes. I saw Eric watching us, a sober expression on his face. It looked something like disbelief and sadness.

Chapter Eight

Logan did put his arm around me to warm me up but also didn't bother saying anything else.

That was all right, though. I had no desire to hear him be so condescending again. With his mouth shut, at least his attitude was turned off.

Although there were more than a dozen other people in the room, Eric was the only one I felt a desire to observe. I wanted to see his reactions to the game. I wanted to know if his eyes ever wandered to me.

When they did, it made me smile inside.

I knew focusing on Eric would cause a lot of trouble, even if no one but me was aware of my admiration.

Despite my urges, I didn't think I should go down that road. Logan and I had always been faithful to each other.

It was only natural that we found others attractive. However, what stirred in me when I saw Eric felt completely different than when I saw anyone else. He wasn't some random hot guy on the street. He was someone I had the inconceivable desire to watch all the time. Not only at the party, either. I had wanted to watch him from the moment I met him. Watching Eric made me want to be near him, which led to thoughts I knew I shouldn't have.

Of course, this induced a lot of unrestrained guilt. Awful, gnawing guilt. I mean, there was no way Logan ever lusted after another woman right in front of me. Probably. Yet I was doing that in front of him.

This meant I had to stop looking at Eric. I just had to. Maybe if I stopped watching Eric, he wouldn't exist for a while. After one last peek.

I finally looked away from him in time to see yet another batter strike out. Maybe I would have been entertained if the Cubs were playing, but I didn't even know who these players were. With a sigh, I realized the chances of this game holding my attention were slim to none. Without baseball to distract me, I knew my mind would begin to wander back to what I'd already fought against. Something about this game and this party had to be interesting, right?

⧗

Not even an hour later, I was annoyed beyond words. All everyone could focus on were the players, the stats, and their predictions. I didn't care who was playing or who won. I'd missed a documentary on the population collapse of indigenous people on a tiny Pacific island for this.

I was so bored, I almost wanted to cry. The only thought I had was to get away from all baseball talk.

Logan took no notice as I carefully removed his arm from around me and headed to the kitchen. I grabbed my gray suede boots and lightweight jacket on the way. Stephanie and her friend Cora were still seated at the island. I quickly realized Loretta and Eric had joined them. The game had been good for at least one thing. I never saw Eric leave the living room.

"Christabel, are you going somewhere?" Loretta asked.

I shook my head while leaning against the counter to put on my shoes. I wanted my boots on as fast as possible without falling over while doing it. "I thought I'd go for a short walk."

"Do you want some company?" This question came from Stephanie.

"I can go, too," Cora added.

"No need, but thanks. I'm just going around the block. I'll be back in a little bit."

As I put on my jacket, I noticed Eric doing the same. Was he planning to take off? I couldn't help but wonder. Maybe he figured if I stepped outside, it could usher in his excuse to go.

"Are you leaving?" My stomach took a tumble at the thought. I wasn't ready for him to disappear yet. We hadn't talked much at all. I didn't want to be there for at least two more hours without him.

"No. I want some fresh air, too," he replied, following me out the back door and closing it behind us.

Yes! That was a *huge* relief.

While we took the stone path that led to the front of the house, I turned to him and said, "I'm a grown woman, you know. You don't need to come with me. I know how to protect myself."

"Would it be so bad if I didn't think you should be out here by yourself at night, even if you do know how to take care of yourself?"

I thought for a moment. "It wouldn't be necessary."

"Well, it doesn't matter, anyway. I'm out here for the quiet. It has nothing to do with you."

He shot a glance at me, and we both smiled.

We reached the main sidewalk in front and turned south, toward the more peaceful part of the block. No barking dogs, little traffic. It was the perfect way to go.

I glanced at Eric in the streetlight. He walked like a different person without a suit on. I mentioned this to him, and he laughed.

"That's because suits suck. I never imagined I'd end up wearing a suit every day to work."

"So, what happened?"

He gave a small shrug. "It's a good job. Good pay, good benefits. I like most of my co-workers. I'm not too keen on management, though."

I looked up at him again. "I thought you were management. Or at least head of your division."

"Uh, well, in a way I am, I suppose. Frankly, I'm where I am now because I don't have to deal with customers all day."

"You don't like people?" I laughed.

"I like people. Just not customers."

"I can understand that. I was a bank teller for about eight months during college and absolutely hated it most of the time. We had several customers who complained to us about everything in their lives, no matter what we were trying to do. Even if a dozen other people were waiting behind them."

"Didn't that frustrate you?"

"Oh, absolutely. But we didn't want to hurt their feelings by telling them to go away. Besides, our boss wouldn't have liked that. A snarky co-worker made someone leave once. Of course, after half an hour in our branch manager's office, she never did that again. I will never forget watching her storm out to the parking lot. It was the first and only time I ever saw her cry."

I took a breath before continuing. "There was one couple especially. After all their transactions were done, the man would talk to us for an hour. I'm not kidding. His wife would stand next to him the entire time, saying things like, 'They don't care about your stories anymore' and 'Arthur, will you shut up already and go to the car?'"

Eric glanced at me. "Wow."

"Yeah. And the thing was, we usually liked his stories even though we never had much time to hear them. He was pretty funny. His wife, though, well... let's just say she was a special treat we could do without."

In the quiet, I heard an owl hooting from a nearby tree. I looked over in an effort to see it and, in the process, caught a small glimpse of the stars. Well, the three or four stars that weren't hidden by clouds.

"You know, it's always made me feel a little dumb that I can't distinguish the constellations in the sky."

"You can't?" he asked.

"Nope. The only ones I know are the Dippers, and even then, I still get them confused sometimes. Do you know any constellations?"

"A few. Some are easier than others. Orion is one of the easiest, for me, anyway." Eric glanced up as well. "I wish I could show you some tonight, but it doesn't look good. I'm not sure the clouds will go away. We might have to stargaze together some other time."

A swift breeze brushed past us, sending a chill through me. I subconsciously tightened my jacket's belt and pulled the sleeves over my hands.

"Are you cold?" Eric's eyes focused on the spaces where my hands had been before they disappeared into what heat I could give them. "Would you like to head back?"

He paused his steps, but I shook my head. We weren't quite to the halfway mark yet. I figured it would be pointless turning around without covering a full block. It sounded like too much backtracking. "I'm okay. I just didn't expect the weather to turn so quickly. It was so nice the other day."

While I spoke, I thought, *Great. I'm talking to him about the weather. Brilliant.*

Once I'd started, I couldn't get out of it. We discussed the coming chilliness and previous warmth until arriving in front of Loretta and David's again. As we silently stared at the house, only the wind and distant cars made any kind of noise. Though Eric and I were quiet, there wasn't any awkwardness to it. Honestly, it was almost perfection.

Eventually, Eric said, "I guess we should go in."

I nodded. "Yeah." Except I wasn't in much of a hurry to. I had exactly what I'd wanted all night.

As far as I could tell, Eric and I were completely alone. There was no one else on the street. If any smokers from the party were outside, they were all in the back. We didn't have any inside witnesses, either. All the curtains in the Mills/Singleton house were closed to keep any errant street or car lights from ruining the prime game-time atmosphere.

Neither Eric nor I moved a foot. I felt a hesitation coming from him. Even still, I expected to see him step forward at any moment. It seemed like the sensible thing to do. He was, after all, a pretty sensible guy.

"Unless..." he said.

I moved my eyes from the house to him. "Unless what?"

"I was thinking that we can keep walking. If you want to. I mean, if you'd like a little more fresh air, or if you're not ready to go inside yet. As long as you aren't too cold."

I thought of the warmth of the house. I thought of the game and the noise. Finally, I thought of Logan.

Looking up at Eric's face, I couldn't hold in a small, guilty smile. "I think a little more air would be nice."

Chapter Nine

We turned north this time, further into the subdivision, heading away from David and Loretta's quiet block. My boots clicked on the sidewalk as Eric and I fell into another conversational lull. I wanted to find something to talk about, but nothing immediately came to mind.

Thankfully, Eric ventured a question of his own. "So, how do you know everyone?"

"How much time do you have?"

He chuckled softly in return.

"No, seriously. This might take a while."

"Take as much time as you need."

I almost fell over from the sexiness in his voice. "Okay, well, I've known everyone for a long time. Stephanie and I were roommates at Northwestern. She had this zestiness about her that was so refreshing."

"Zestiness?" Eric asked with a raised eyebrow.

"What? It's a word."

He stared at me, eyebrow still up.

I laughed. "Okay, it's my word. But it suits her. Once she and I started hanging out more, I got to know Loretta better. That's how I met David, of course. Then about a year ago, Steph met Cora while with friends somewhere. Jesse, by the way, is also Logan's best friend and has been for a long time. Logan and Jesse met when we were all thirteen. They played baseball together. Figures, right?" I stopped for a second, realizing my nervous babbling had gotten way out of control.

Eric's face then took on an odd expression. "So, Logan is your boyfriend."

I sucked in a breath but couldn't seem to let it out. "He is." I couldn't bring myself to look at Eric. How had I not expected him to ask about Logan? It felt like a moment when I needed to say more, but nothing parted my lips.

Eric and I quietly wandered on for a few minutes. As we turned a corner, a rather large German shepherd rushed to the side of its fence, roaring a deep bark with all its might. I screeched and jumped about ten feet in the air. I then took a few very large steps back before realizing the dog was inside the fence, not outside.

I quickly looked to Eric, who laughed.

"Are you okay, Christabel?" I couldn't read the expression in his eyes, but his face displayed a half-smile full of amusement.

"Yeah. I'm fine," I scoffed with a wave of the hand.

No, I did not just jump out of my skin. No, my heart is not thumping near breaking point. And no, I was not terrified by the giant, snarling beast. If only I had enough air in my lungs to actually say all this.

"You sure? The dog didn't scare you?"

"No! Of course not." I faked a laugh. A pretty ridiculous one, I have to say. "It was unexpected, that's all."

"Okay. If you say so." He patiently waited for me to join him again, temporarily taking the part of sidewalk closest to the shepherd before moving to the other side to avoid some overgrown tree limbs.

I felt the need to turn the situation around somehow. I needed to return to my previously strong, "I am woman/hear me roar" attitude. "I don't scare all that easily, you know."

"You don't?" There was that expression in his eyes again. I thought I understood it this time. It looked like entertainment. I was like a happy clown to him. Loud, excited, jumpy, playful. No wonder he couldn't help but laugh at me and my feeble attempt at asserting my bravery.

"Well, maybe a little." I couldn't hold in a sheepish grin as he moved his eyes to me. "Besides, it wasn't that I was scared, more that I was startled. I do not like being startled."

"I'll have to remember that." He smiled before speaking again. "You know, I find it interesting how life is sometimes."

"What do you mean?"

"Random things. Events that seem so insignificant in the moment. When you meet a person, you never expect how important they might be to you one day. Friend. Lover. Spouse." He glanced my way, sending a flutter through me.

I turned my face away to hide the blush that quickly spread across my cheeks. I was doing my best to remind myself that I should only think of Eric as a friend, but he wasn't making it easy for me. He had me wanting to know everything I could about him, and also everything I shouldn't. I wanted to hear his thoughts about so many things. Logan never had the kind of insights that Eric had. Eric was such a different man from my boyfriend.

I knew what I had to do. I had to change the subject before things started down a very wrong path. *Again.*

"I'm surprised you managed to pull yourself away from the game so easily. Logan never would. He's as obsessed with the game as the others are. Wait, I take that back. Logan is definitely more obsessed about baseball than the others. He is more obsessed than anyone I know."

"I'm not much of a sports guy. I'm more into cars, trucks, that kind of thing."

"Really?" That was a little hard to believe. Even the car guys I knew were still sports fans. "You mean you never even watch the Luvabulls?"

"The who?"

I laughed. "Wow. Okay. You honestly don't watch sports, do you? The cheerleaders for the Bulls..."

A slight glint of recognition lit up in his eyes. "Oh, right. Yeah, I think I've seen them before."

"Huh. You're probably the only warm-blooded Chicago-area man I know of that has never attended a Bulls game in order to see them gyrate around. A few guys from my agency bought season tickets just to see the Luvabulls dance."

Eric shrugged a "That's nice" answer, like it would never occur to him to do such a thing.

"Well, anyway, I actually wanted to be a Luvabull when I was younger. For a whole five weeks, I believe, which was a long time for me back then."

"Nothing lasted beyond that?"

"Not really. Maybe my ballerina phase, but that's about it. Nothing stuck until high school. I tried out for the Luvabulls once. About two years ago, they held open auditions for one lucky fan to win a chance to perform with them at a Bulls game. A co-worker and I tried out as a joke."

It was Jetta's idea. I thought there was no way in the world we would ever be picked. She agreed but also reminded me that it was one of those once-in-a-lifetime things.

"A joke?"

"Well, I say 'joke,' but we gave it an honest effort. To the best of our abilities, anyway. We never made it past the first round."

Eric gave a slight headshake. "Too bad. I'd watch them if you were on the squad."

Mmm. I was blushing galore. I almost couldn't walk straight, imagining Eric watching me dance around in a curve-hugging outfit. Would he be impressed? Would the sight of me make him smile? Would he—

Okay, that's enough. Continuing that last thought would have sent me into a nosedive of wondering how much Eric would be turned on by Christabel the Luvabull. I willed my heart rate and breathing to slow back down to normal.

Focus! Must focus. Sports. I cleared my throat. "So, you don't watch any games ever? Not even football?"

"Not really. I don't care that much about sports. I'd rather fix up old cars in my spare time. Whenever I'm lucky enough to have any. There hasn't been much of that lately."

I nodded slightly in agreement. "I know how you feel. Work sort of takes over, doesn't it?"

"Far too often."

"Then you're left with no time for the things you love."

"Or the people." Eric shot a look my way.

More flutters in my heart, my stomach, my *entire* body.

"So, uh, what kind of cars do you like?" I asked as we turned a corner.

"Dodges. And trucks more than cars."

"Nice-looking ones?" Not that I had ever seen a truck I really liked the look of, but maybe that was just me.

"Uh, well, really ugly, square ones. But I like them."

"Fixing ugly, square trucks, huh?" I moved my eyes to him. "For some reason, I can't picture you doing something like that. It doesn't seem like that would be your hobby."

"Oh, yeah?" He smiled in return. "Then what does?"

I took a longer look at him and watched as he easily avoided the protruding branch of a still-green leafy shrub. On one hand, he was the sleek business professional; on the other, a laidback truck enthusiast. He was such a mystery to me. "Honestly? I'm not sure."

He flashed a grin but didn't reply.

"So, if you aren't into baseball, why go to a baseball-themed party?"

"I don't know. I thought it might be fun. David is a pretty cool guy."

"Yes, he is. He's the best."

"And Logan," he added.

"Oh, yes. Logan, too. Of course."

Oops! I'd forgotten all about Logan.

In order to not feel like such a crappy girlfriend, I was about to tell Eric all the wonderful qualities Logan possessed. But I noticed I couldn't see as well as I had been able to. I looked up and realized the streetlights in this area were out. Eric and I were in a virtual blackness, but going back the way we came would have more than doubled the time of our already lengthy walk. We weren't even in the subdivision anymore. There was no other choice but to continue on the sidewalk, under the railroad bridge.

I'd blindly stumbled a few steps when I felt Eric's ever-so-slightly beat-up hand on my own, strong and reassuring.

As surprising as it was for him to take my hand, I never felt the urge to pull away. I didn't always admit when I needed people, but I definitely needed him. And I loved that he knew that without me having to tell him. He carefully guided me in the dark, gently calling out directions every so often to avoid this crack or that broken bit, keeping me on a stable path. I tried to focus on my feet, but all I could think about was how perfectly my hand fit inside Eric's.

I'd felt little sparks when we first shook hands at the conference. This time, the sparks felt like fireworks in the most wonderful way. These fireworks had all the power of real ones.

I could tell Eric felt it, too. As we walked in the darkness, he gave my hand a small squeeze. It wasn't a "your hand is slipping from mine" squeeze, a "we're almost there" one, or even an "I'm not ready to let go yet" one. It was the kind that a boyfriend would give his girlfriend just because, just to let her know that he was happy in that moment holding her hand and having her close. I liked it so much that I squeezed Eric's hand in return without thinking. Then the guilt just about knocked me off my feet.

It was a guilt that never fully went away. I mean, honestly, I hadn't done anything wrong. Not really. I just had to figure out what to do about these feelings for Eric.

Once our path was illuminated by streetlights again, I looked at Eric's hand still in my own. His warmth had spread through my hand into my body, taking off the chill I'd felt from the wind. Reluctantly, and quite awkwardly, I released my hand from his in order to fix my hair.

Of course, there was nothing wrong with my hair. I didn't know how to comfortably let go. There was that pesky problem of wanting to hold on forever.

Eric quickly ran a hand through his own hair. He cleared his throat then stammered, "Talking. You were talking, right? Were you...You were going to say something. What was it?"

I tightened my jacket around my waist, pulling my hands into the sleeves again. "I have no idea," I lied.

"Maybe we should talk about something else," Eric said slowly.

I grinned. "Good idea."

"So, tell me more about your job."

"What would you like to know?" I asked.

"Well, I already know you started when you were fifteen. What have you done recently?"

"Anything I'm tasked to do. Do you remember the online commercial with the sharks grilling hot dogs?"

Eric thought for a moment. "Yeah, I saw it a few times."

I smiled at him. "That was mine."

"Really?" His voice was happy and enthusiastic.

"Yep. I wrote all the copy for it. It was my all-time favorite creation."

"I can see why."

I turned to my walking partner again. "Okay, your turn."

We made it back to Loretta and David's as Eric was finishing his story about a manager from his old job years before. The man absolutely drove Eric crazy, and he wasn't afraid to tell him so. His manager hated being confronted with his own mistakes. Eric told me that in the end, after all the yelling and arm waiving, the guy would finally admit he was wrong. He'd fix the problems he caused, and everything would be okay—until the whole thing started over again about a new issue. And on it went.

The best part of the story was Eric's imitation of his former manager. Arms flailing frantically about, eyes bugged out, face flushed. It was perfect.

We entered the door to the kitchen in a laughing fit, only to be overwhelmed with questions from Loretta. "Where have you been? We were worried about you! What took so long? You've been gone for over two hours!"

As far as I could tell, no one else was panicked. I assumed Loretta was the only worried person in the house. Leave it to a stay-at-home mom of three kids to act like a mother hen with everyone else. She turned to Eric. "I thought you left."

After taking a quick glance at the kitchen clock, I told her, "We're sorry." I did my best to look regretful while not actually regretting my time with Eric. "We didn't realize we were gone for so long."

Loretta sighed. "Take your phone with you next time."

"I have my phone with me," I said, confused.

I quickly pulled my cell phone out of my inside jacket pocket. The screen was black. I powered it on. Four missed calls, two voice messages, and three unread texts, all within the last hour. Then I remembered turning off my phone.

"I'm sorry," I told Loretta again.

She silently stalked off to the living room.

Eric leaned closer to me. "I'll walk with you again anytime."

Talk about piercing my soul.

Out of the corner of my eye, I noticed Cora watching us. Eric seemed to notice her, too, and looked uncomfortable. That was not good for several reasons. Cora, I knew, would report back to Stephanie, and therefore everyone, that she saw me getting cozy with a man who wasn't Logan. This particular group of friends often commented on my disastrous choices in men. Logan was the first one they all agreed was good for me. Being suspected of betraying both Logan and their trust in me was something I did not want to deal with.

Without needing to say a thing, Eric and I decided to follow Loretta's lead and head to the living room. We'd already removed our shoes at the back door. I returned my jacket to the coat rack by the wall closest to the front door. I rejoined Logan on the sofa, my spot next to him still available. He wrapped his arm around me once more, and I snuggled into him.

"Why are you so cold?" he asked, actually *turning away from the game* to look at me.

It might have been the first time in his entire life he looked somewhere other than the field while the ball was still in play.

My heart almost stopped from shock. My jaw certainly dropped. It took a moment for it to register that he was waiting for an answer. "I stepped outside for a bit."

"Oh, yeah. Loretta asked me about that. I told her I was sure you were fine. Were you really outside that long by yourself?"

I reflexively cleared my throat. "Uh, no." I tried lowering my voice, but it had a mind of its own and rose about an octave as I spoke. "Actually, Eric was with me. David's friend."

Logan nodded, an unreadable expression on his face. "You didn't want to watch the game?"

"I did. It just felt a bit stuffy in here. I needed some fresh air. Then it got really cold out there."

"Come here, then," Logan told me, gently pulling me closer. I was almost in his lap now, both his arms holding me tight. He began to lightly rub my arms, thighs, and hands, passing on what heat he could.

It was moments like this that made me wonder why I ever questioned his attentiveness.

I softly kissed Logan's cheek, and we turned back to the game. As I did so, I spotted Eric watching us.

There was an obvious difference in the way Cora watched Eric and me, and the way Eric watched Logan and me. I knew Cora was just being nosy. However, Eric's face conveyed a different and much more profound reason.

In order to control the fluttering that quickly reappeared, I looked at Logan again. "Hey, do you think we can—"

"We're still in the inning, baby," he said shortly, his eyes glued to the screen.

My open window had slammed shut and locked itself.

Chapter Ten

"A home run! No one ever expects that guy to hit a home run. Groundouts, usually. A sacrifice bunt, maybe. But never a home run. And with two runners already in scoring position, no less. Very impressive. I wasn't sure the guy had it in him. By the second strike, I thought it was all over. He'd fly out or something, the inning would end, and they would have to work even harder the next inning."

Logan and I were on our way back to my apartment. He raved on and on about how fantastic his pick had played. I saw them win the game, but I had no idea how they got to that point. Before I left the living room for my walk, Logan's team was down by five runs in the second inning and their pitching prospects weren't looking good.

"And that five-four-three play in the sixth was incredible. At first, it didn't look like they'd get it. Do you remember that?" He glanced at me with such excitement in his eyes.

"Uh, no, I didn't actually see that one. I was outside." Honestly, I hadn't witnessed a single play he talked about.

Even those I'm sure happened while I remained in the living room. Had my mind blanked out that much?

Of course it had, I told myself. *There is no other explanation for my absence of memory.*

"Oh. Well, it was great. It had to be one of the best plays of the game. That part in the eighth was pretty great, too. And I knew they would win. They couldn't lose with their lead-off man being so healthy again."

Logan continued on about the game, and while I didn't care all that much about who won or lost, I tried to be interested for his sake. There was a certain quality to his happiness that made it impossible not to want to feel the same way. His entire face lit up. The tone of his voice was lively and maybe a little bubbly. His eyes even danced with glee.

Unfortunately, Eric was still on my mind. It was like a constant battle in my head. One side of me pushed him away as hard as it could. The other held a death grip on his arm and refused to let go. I had no idea how to get this struggle under control.

I looked at my boyfriend again, watching the glow on his face as he described his emotions during the tense final inning. "I couldn't believe it! He leapt about five feet in the air. Everything depended on that catch. *Everything.* And I just kept wondering how the hell he did it. It was incredible!"

I smiled the best I could, but it wasn't as convincing as I thought.

"What's wrong, Christabel?" he asked, his beautifully happy face slowly crinkling into worry. We paused at a stoplight, and he turned to me. "Are you okay?"

I had no clue what to say. How was I supposed to explain what was going through my mind? I didn't even know what was happening in there. It was all such a jumble of Logan, Eric, baseball stats I didn't care about, and so much randomness it wasn't even funny.

The only thing I was certain of was that I just couldn't be falling for a guy I barely knew. It was crazy to think I might have been.

It had been a huge step for Logan to look away from the game. Like I said, he had never done that before. Regardless of what happened after that, or even before, it still showed that Logan cared about me. And the knowledge of what being around Eric did to me would have been more than even Logan could handle.

I caught his eyes and smiled as genuinely as possible. "I'm okay. Really. I have a bit of a headache. A lot of things on my mind."

We reached my apartment building. After parking, Logan and I exited the car. The night had gotten colder. The wind speed had increased as well, adding to the chill. Logan took my hand as he slowly walked me inside and upstairs.

I lived on the second floor of a three-story brick building from the 1920s. No one bothered adding elevators, which I loved at first because the stunning molding on the staircase enhanced the building's charm. The adoration began to wear off after countless trips hauling things up the stairs, down the stairs, up the stairs, and so on. Adding larger furniture pieces to my apartment was a horror I never wanted to experience again. I knew if I ever had to move out, I'd totally leave the place fully furnished. My gift to the new renters in order to avoid anyone else going through that nightmare.

In the empty hallway outside my door, I stood up on my tiptoes and softly kissed Logan's lips.

Before we dated, I never would have suspected Logan of being a great kisser. Don't ask me why. It might have been simply because he was my friend; no more, no less.

Then he kissed me for the first time. Well, for the second time, technically, because the first kiss caught me off-guard and therefore wasn't as great. Totally my fault, though. I even giggled during and after the first kiss. Everything changed with those kisses. After our lips first met, I could no longer look at Logan as my friend, an altered state I happily accepted.

He was more than willing to kiss me in return this September night. His kisses were soft at first, like always, but soon became much more passionate. Logan leaned into me, a hand on my waist and another in my hair. Pressing me against the door with his entire body, he tantalizingly moved his mouth slowly and deliberately across my cheek and down my neck.

The fluttering was back again. It was a little different this time, but still as intense. So was the pounding of my heart.

Wrapping my arms around his muscular back, I closed my eyes and enjoyed the feel of him for a moment. I really, *really* loved his kisses, no matter where or how his lips touched me. They put me in such a beautiful, almost relaxed state. I squeezed Logan a little tighter.

"You smell so sweet," he whispered, his lips briefly grazing my ear. "What is it?"

"My perfume," I replied breathlessly. "Pomegranate mango."

Logan's voice was as breathless in return. "Smells good enough to eat."

I laughed, and he returned to his kissing. He moved his other hand up to my hair, absently playing with a curl here or there.

I wanted to run my hands through Logan's short, slightly wavy hair as well, but that would have been pointless. Not only was it a little crunchy from his gel, but he hated when I messed up his hair.

He owned and regularly used more gel, mousse, and hair spray than I could ever fathom. Sometimes, if he was in a hurry, he'd quickly rub in this no-name cheap stuff that made his hair crunchy and immoveable. Usually, though, he bought and used with great deliberation fairly higher-end products that left his hair soft and flexible with perfect hold. Not one strand ever shifted out of its designated place.

I thought about this for all of five seconds, though, because Logan was still busy sending tingles all through me.

"Logan?" I eventually said, forcing my eyes open once more.

"Hmm?" he replied from my collarbone.

Both of his hands were around my waist, but he quickly slipped one under my shirt, right above my hip. He softly rubbed my hip bone with his thumb, something he knew I loved. His skin was hot on mine, a sweet warmth I welcomed to permeate into the rest of me. I relaxed against the door as Logan began sliding his hand up my side.

I thought a moment.

"Logan," I repeated in a slightly firmer tone.

He leaned back, moving his eyes up to meet mine. I tried to steady my breathing as he stared into me. "Are you sure?" he finally asked.

I nodded slowly. "Yeah. I'm sure."

With furrowed brows and a frowning mouth, he said, "We could just sleep. It is possible for two people to sleep together and not have sex."

"You and I both know we wouldn't end up sleeping."

"Most girlfriends would at least invite me in for coffee or a drink or something."

I sighed. He was giving me a harder time than usual about this. "Good night," I told him before giving him a quick kiss on the lips.

Logan gave a sigh, removing his hands from me. "All right. I'll see you tomorrow?"

"Absolutely," I smiled.

The "tomorrow" Logan mentioned was our make-up day for the canceled date. I so couldn't wait for it. After a Saturday meeting, I would definitely need some boyfriend time. Since we had never rescheduled a date so quickly, I wanted to seize the moment before something else came up to delay it again.

I realized Logan hadn't moved his feet yet. It almost seemed like he was frozen to the floor. As he stood in front of me, Logan rubbed the back of his neck. He wouldn't make eye contact. His happiness was shadowed over by something.

Logan wasn't usually this serious. I felt like I should help him, but I didn't know how. Though we both opened our mouths, only his voice came out.

"Hey, Christabel? I... I wanted to, um... I, uh..." He stopped, and I looked at him with wonder.

He was a very sure man, as far as speaking was concerned. If he started a sentence, he finished it, no stopping, ceasing, or stalling. No verbal stumbles at all. Everything was spoken with clear certainty. This stuttering was a strange thing to hear him do.

"You what?" I asked in a gentle tone, putting my hand on his arm. "What is it?"

Logan quickly shook his head. "Uh, nothing. It's nothing."

While he wasn't physically pulling away, he was starting to shut me out. I had no idea how to stop it. "Are you sure? Because—"

"Everything's okay. Don't worry about it."

"Logan—"

"Hey." He brushed the back of his fingers on my cheek. "It's okay. Nothing important."

"That's it?" His face told me nothing. Neither did his eyes. What in the world was he trying to do to me?

He nodded. "That's it." He sighed again before giving me a quick kiss. "Good night, babe."

I didn't know what to think about that, but at any rate, his confident demeanor was back. I blindly took that as a good sign and ignored how swiftly it all happened. I assumed he would have told me if it really was important. Possibly.

"Good night," I told him. There wasn't much else for me to do. I entered my apartment as Logan headed for the stairs.

In addition to Logan's odd behavior, I knew how disappointed he was that I didn't invite him in. Logan and I had never had sex. Not with each other, anyway.

When I was eighteen, I made the mistake of sleeping with my slightly older boyfriend, Brandon, because I thought he loved me. At least, he always told me he did every day in every conversation.

Except he didn't. Our relationship was all about him. Anything, everything. Whatever Brandon wanted, whenever he wanted it. It was all about making him happy. It didn't matter that I was miserable. He said he cared, but he never, ever showed it. There was absolutely zero proof that I meant more to him than, say, a used tissue or a clump of mud stuck in his boot. And believe me, the sex was *far* from magical enough to make up for everything else.

He broke up with me when he got bored. I cried for days afterward then fell into a depression that lasted for months. I felt so used and so betrayed. It made me sick to my stomach remembering what I gave up for him. What especially bothered me was that he never even acknowledged any of it. Not my love for him or any sacrifice I made. He just discarded me like I'd been a piece of lint he picked off his sweater.

I'd vowed right then that I wouldn't have sex again unless I was absolutely certain it was with *the* guy for me. The one to love me no matter what. The one to marry me.

After nearly eight years, the hurt from that "relationship" still hung around. I regretted Brandon and all that he reminded me of. Why would I bother doing it or even think about doing it with Logan, a guy I wasn't in love with?

I knew some would say that we were adults. Sex was just something adults did when in relationships. I had been told this several times by both my friends—*cough* Jetta *cough*—and one or two of Logan's. Benefits, statistics, even personal opinions. And most of it came down to that one simple fact.

Their reasoning just didn't cut it for me. I thought it was stupid to make such a huge decision based on the opinions of other people.

The absence of sex in our relationship bothered Logan sometimes. In the end, though, he respected me enough to kiss me good night and go to bed alone, whether or not he was happy about it. I refused to do it solely for the purpose of making Logan feel better.

After removing my jacket and boots, I pulled out my phone in order to charge it. While it was in my hand, I decided to go through my unread text messages. There was one from Jetta. I sent a quick message to her and started looking for my charger. A new text from her arrived almost immediately.

Jetta: Why are you answering me now? Where is Logan?

Me: He left.

I looked at the screen and read Jetta's next text.

Jetta: ???

Yeah. Jetta really didn't understand.

I shuffled into the kitchen for a drink of water. Fridge door closed and water glass emptied, I returned to the living room to lock the door. Then I headed to my tiny bathroom to wash up for bed.

Fresh and makeup free, I crossed the hall into my bedroom, quickly stripping down in order to crawl into my favorite blue plaid pajamas. I thought a cold night deserved warm flannel to keep it at bay. After checking my alarm for the morning, I plopped into bed, wrapping all the blankets around me. In the darkness, I listened to the hum of my freezer's defrost cycle as I began drifting off to sleep.

The last thing that flashed through my mind was Eric's face.

Chapter Eleven

To my delight, Eric attended all the rest of David and Loretta's World Series parties, as did I. It took a lot of finagling and promising Jetta the world if she would help be out, but I managed. I told myself it was all for Logan. He was, after all, responding faster to my texts than he had in months.

Logan began tagging me on social media as well, with captions of "I miss you" and "happy together" on pictures of us. Then he started tagging me on pics and videos of adorable baby animals and other things he knew I liked. It was a layer to our relationship that we'd never had before. At one point, I had more notifications from him than I could read through in a few minutes.

When my phone dinged in the middle of one lunch break, I was surprised it wasn't a text from my boyfriend.

Loretta: You busy this Sunday?

Me: All free. What's going on?

Loretta: David suggested a birthday dinner for Eric.

It's Eric's birthday? I opened my social media apps, one by one, and searched for Eric to find some kind of confirmation. He wasn't on any of them.

Me: When is Eric's birthday?

I used only one question mark, but the giddy part of me wanted to use five.

Loretta: Tomorrow. We're thinking of taking him to that burger place we all went to for David's birthday. David, Eric, a few of their co-workers, me, you, and Logan.

I wanted to do a happy dance right there on my desk.

Me: That's fine. Have you asked Logan yet?

Loretta: David texted him earlier but hasn't heard back yet.

Me: Don't worry. I'll take care of it.

I couldn't call Logan fast enough. "So, where would you like to meet?" I asked once I'd explained the plan.

Logan didn't answer right away. "We hardly know the guy."

"Logan, we've been hanging out with him for weeks now, and I see him nearly every day at work." *Oops.* I wasn't sure I told Logan that part before. "Eric is more our friend now than just David's."

He again stayed quiet for a few moments. "If you really want to."

"I do," I answered right away. Then I cleared my throat in an attempt to cool my excitement. "I mean, it'll be great to see our friends and eat delicious food."

"We do that, anyway, but sure."

I might not have wholly convinced him, but he agreed to go all the same.

Three more days until the dinner. I couldn't wait!

Sunday afternoon, hours before meeting time, I flipped through all the clothes in my closet, wondering how to look my best without it being obvious that I was trying to. I eventually decided on soft black leggings, low V-neck red knit sweater, and gray ankle boots. Not too fancy. Enough to make the kind of statement I was going for.

Logan grinned when I opened the door for him. "Ready?" he asked.

We were the first to arrive at the restaurant, followed closely after by Eric.

"Hey! Happy birthday!" I said as soon as I saw him.

"Thanks." Eric gave me a smile. "Hey, Logan."

"Hey, man."

All three of us grew quiet. I didn't know what to say to cut through the awkwardness. The only thing I could think of was a question about the ad campaign.

"It's great. Joe really knows what he's doing."

I nodded in agreement. "He does. He's the best I've ever worked with, outside of Jetta."

"Wait," Logan said, turning to me. "You aren't on that campaign? But you two see each other every day?"

"My bosses insist on having meetings every day at Madison. Christabel and I run into each other in the hallway and elevators a lot."

"You know how Mari is about meetings," I added.

Logan's crinkled face told me he didn't believe me. Thankfully, David, Loretta, and the co-workers arrived shortly after.

While eating dinner, Eric mentioned the hayrides he used to have for his birthdays.

"In the beginning of November?" Loretta asked.

Eric smiled. "That's what warm clothes and boots are for."

"I've never been on a hayride," I told him.

"We always did bonfires, too. " Eric's gaze held mine. "I think you'd really like it."

I beamed at him. "I think I would. Might have to join you sometime."

Logan swiped a few sweet potato fries from my plate.

I turned to see him grinning. "You weren't going to eat those, were you?" he asked in a teasing tone.

"Not if you share your cheese fries with me."

He solemnly picked up a cheese fry from his plate and moved it to my mouth. I let him feed it to me, both of us smiling at each other after my first bite. I didn't hear much of the conversation after that. Logan kept most of my attention.

When it was time to leave, we all gathered near the exit doors to say goodbye. Although Logan was still trying to keep my thoughts and conversation engaged by only him, I managed to say a final happy birthday to Eric.

"I hope you had a great dinner," I added.

His eyes flicked away before returning to meet mine. "It was the best I could hope for, all things considered."

"Because you miss being down on the farm?" Logan asked him.

His words were harmless, but I heard the condescension in his tone.

Eric looked at Logan and opened his mouth. But he didn't say anything. Only a few seconds passed before he closed his mouth again.

Loretta took the opportunity to herd us all outside to our vehicles, promising another party soon. Football season had already shifted into gear. It was another favorite sport of the group and another reason to celebrate all winter long.

I only had to wait until the next morning to see Eric again.

"Thanks for coming last night," he told me after we literally bumped into each other in the conference room corridor.

I smiled. "You don't have to thank me. I wanted to be there." More than I could admit to anyone.

He stepped around Robert, who'd walked in between us, and came closer to me. "So, you've really never been on a hayride?"

I laughed. "Evanston isn't exactly the hayride capital of the world. Neither is Oak Park."

"Where you live now?" he asked.

"You got it."

Joe walked over to us. "Sorry, Griff. Mari wants us back in there. She has a new plan for the timeline."

I turned to Joe. "What about her meeting with my team?"

He shrugged. "Don't know. She didn't go into detail, per usual."

I gave a hearty sigh. "Great. That's just great."

"I'm not happy about it, either," Joe told me.

Eric glanced back and forth between us. "Sorry, Fuller, but I don't think we can do that."

"Joe," we heard Mari's voice call.

All three of us moved our bodies to look over at her.

"Wait here," Eric whispered to me before he and Joe headed over to Mari.

I could only see her face, not theirs. She smiled, relaxed at first. Then her smile grew taut and flat. After nodding a few times, she shook Eric's hand and motioned for me to join her in the conference room. She then stalked off into that room, most likely boiling inside.

I hurried over to Eric. "I can't believe you just did that for me," I whispered to him once Joe strolled over to the nearest elevator.

Eric shook his head. "I don't know what you're talking about." Then came his sly smile.

"Thank you for saving my meeting." Then I rushed into the room before Mari yelled for me.

As embarrassing and demanding as my boss was, Eric had managed her like a pro. He took a risk to help me. No one except Jetta had done anything close to that before. It didn't matter that he couldn't admit it.

When our meeting was over, I pulled Jetta aside to tell her what happened with Eric. "He saved us from having to reschedule everything."

She raised her eyebrows. "Damn. How did Mari not lose her shit over that?"

I grinned. "Don't know, don't care. We get to stay on track, thanks to Eric. That's all I need to know."

"Oh, I'm sure you'd like to know more than that."

I looked up to see her smirk. While rolling my eyes, I said as casually as I could, "You think that about everyone."

She had no idea how correct she was. In some ways, anyway.

Though I usually didn't want sex or even think about it, this didn't stop me from dreaming about it. What could I say? I was asleep at the time so it wasn't like I had any control.

Unfortunately for Logan, the most vivid dreams weren't about him. They were rather graphic ones about Eric. Those dreams turned me into a red-faced, giggling idiot for weeks afterward whenever I saw Eric, both at work and at all those parties.

I stuttered when talking to him. I could barely look him in those gorgeous turquoise eyes. It was so excruciating. All it took was one grin of his to set me off again.

One time, he tucked a stray hair of mine behind my ear because my hands were full, and I seriously leaned in to kiss him. Forgetting, of course, this was real life, not a dream, and I had no right to kiss Eric. I caught myself and stopped before I got too close. I had only moved an inch or so, but it was enough to make me blush so hard I thought my cheeks might set the rest of my face on fire. It was also enough to cause Eric's eyes to grow wide, his pupils to dilate, and his mouth to slide into a smile.

I made the huge mistake of telling Jetta about the dreams. "So, was it a sex dream you had in the office, or was it dream sex that took place in the office?"

"Dream sex in the office."

She looked at my desk on which she sat. "Here?"

"Yep."

She looked over at hers. "There?"

"Of course not. No one's desk but my own. Eh, well, and Mari's, but in my defense, it was mine in the dream."

Jetta, fascinated by this, spent the rest of the day asking me, "Here? Did you do it here? There?" No matter where we went and no matter how many times I asked her to stop.

"I am never telling you anything again," I huffed.

She smiled. "Yes, you will. You love me. Probably not as much as you loved that dream. Here?" She whispered as we entered the conference room.

I gave her a knowing smile.

I received a call from Logan later on. "How's guys' night going?" I asked while re-reading the copy I'd just finished typing.

"Canceled," he said.

I took a second to blink away the eye strain I was experiencing. "What do you mean by canceled? Aren't you with Jesse?"

"No. That's why I've been trying to get ahold of you today. I thought we could have a date night."

"Oh." Realizing my voice sounded flat, I added, "Oh! That's so sweet of you, but it's already almost eight o'clock now."

"It's okay." His voice was soft. "I can meet you at the agency. We can go wherever you'd like."

"Honestly, Logan, when I'm done here, I just want to go home."

"We can do that, too. I can come over and hang out with you, and you know I don't care if you change into your pajamas."

I took in a deep breath but held off on the sigh. "Logan, I probably won't be out of here for another hour or two."

"That's okay."

When I didn't reply, he added, "Please, Christabel."

"All right," I relented. "I'll text you when I get home."

I could have left right then. I could have texted him when I left work but hadn't yet made the drive home. Only, neither of these options appealed to me.

Nearly an hour-and-a-half later, Logan and I settled onto my sofa and turned on the most recent series we'd been binge-watching. Just about thirty minutes passed, not even an entire episode, when I pulled myself out from Logan's cuddle and stood.

He moved his eyes away from the screen and up to me before asking, "What's going on?"

"I'm sorry. We've been so swamped at work. I really need to sleep right now."

Logan stood and gave me a gentle kiss on the forehead. "I understand. Call you tomorrow."

I locked the door after he left then grabbed my phone from my purse.

Me: How's the bar-hopping going? What number are you on now?

Jetta: Number 1 still. Jules found a guy she swears is a keeper.

Me: You disagree?

Jetta: Oh hell yes

I laughed out loud.

Jetta: Logan gone yet?

Me: Yep

Jetta: How?

Me: Told him I'm going to sleep.

Jetta: Look at you, lying like a boss.

I sent her the eye roll emoji.

Me: Not lying. Just not as tired as I was. Tell me about the guy Jules now loves whom you hate.

My bestie and I spent the next hour dishing on the hot guys at bar number one—which she and her sister never left—and whose taste in men was the worst.

That next Tuesday, I was sitting at my desk, attempting to arrange random ideas I'd come up with about a client that was about to begin a new ad campaign. I knew I should have been working on my current client but couldn't focus. At least I was trying to work on something. I could just as easily have been filling out a crossword puzzle or checking the next week's weather report.

We used to be so free before Mari started. When experiencing a mental block, we could leave our desks, even the building. There was an entire floor devoted to our relaxation. It contained several lounges, a movie room, a game room, a snack bar, and a library. Almost anything we might need to clear our heads and reenergize ourselves was encouraged. Our old CD knew the benefits that came with a change of scenery. An office full of bored creatives leads to boring concepts.

Mari didn't understand this. While she had an unbelievably creative brain, she also had this rigid, uptight side to her that neither relaxed nor relented. A month before, Mari decided to switch out the third copywriter on my team with Robert, who was a senior copywriter.

Robert just *loved* the fact that Mari was in charge. He deemed the previous CD too lax on rules. How he got started in copywriting I never understood. To me, he was way too neurotic to be a creative. He would have been better suited for life as a lawyer or a government employee if not for his genius campaigns. As brilliant as he was, Robert stuck to very hawkish-style philosophies about us staying at our desks and doing what we were told. No questioning "authority," as in the directors or the clients.

Robert believed in catering to the clients when sometimes we had to tell *them* what they needed, not the other way around. There was also the fact that Robert was the adult version of a hall monitor. An irritating, irritable hall monitor.

He stopped in front of my desk as I was trying to focus. "You're working on our project, right?"

"Of course, I am," I told him with a sigh.

"Do you need me to help you?"

I took this as, "Do you need me holding your hand through this whole process since you clearly don't know what you are doing?"

"Nope. I'm doing great. How about you?" I asked him.

"I'm good," he replied.

I watched him step a little closer, obviously checking to see if I was indeed keeping busy with our project. Thank God I'd talked myself out of googling Eric for fun.

Why the heck would Mari feel the need to stick Jetta and me with the grown-up tattletale? There was only one reason I could think of: Mari had lost confidence in our abilities.

As Robert finally began to walk away, I gave him a fake smile while randomly typing letters on my computer keyboard. I knew he couldn't see the screen from his position. When he was gone, I erased everything I'd typed and returned to my old handwritten notes. I also surreptitiously pulled out my cell phone.

Me: We should have quit when Georgina left.

Jetta: We tried, remember? I wish she could have taken us cuz no one else was hiring.

I was busy typing up those random ideas for my long-term client when I heard a man's familiar voice speaking to me. I looked up to see Eric standing in front of my desk. There was a nice sheen to his brown hair. His tie was loosened and his jacket off, sure signs he'd just left a meeting. He held his jacket, coat, and briefcase in his hands.

"Hi." I smiled.

"Hey, Christabel." He grinned in return.

Gosh. Just hearing Eric say my name made my body tingle.

Ever the professional, and terrified that Mari or Robert could be watching, I stopped typing and asked, "Is there something I can help you with?"

"Actually, I don't have to be back at my office for a while, so I was wondering if you'd like to have lunch with me. If you're not too busy."

"She's not busy," Jetta called from her own desk. We glanced over at her, and then Eric looked back at me with a wide smile.

I wanted to be annoyed with Jetta. We had planned to eat lunch together. But I knew exactly what she would say: "You and I can eat lunch together anytime. You don't always have that chance with Eric."

I definitely agreed with her. Then worry popped into my head. What if Mari or Robert noticed I was gone? It was earlier than I normally lunched. But when would I be able to have lunch with Eric like this?

"I guess I'm not busy," I replied to him with a grin.

"So, you'll join me?"

"Sure."

He instantly perked up at my answer.

I grabbed my black canvas bag and crimson wool coat from under my desk. While my computer shut down, I slid my arms through the coat's sleeves and loosely re-wrapped my striped scarf around my neck. Eric put on his own jacket and coat, setting his briefcase on my desk to do so.

As we passed Jetta's desk to head for the elevator, I cast another glance her way, silently telling her how pleasantly surprised I was about Eric's lunch invite.

I mean, this wasn't our first lunch together. More like our fifteenth. However, we'd never been alone. We were always in a combined group of co-workers or friends. To be alone with Eric was thrilling.

Jetta, in turn, smiled and raised her eyebrows at me as if to say she was happily surprised as well.

I stopped by her desk. "If Mari asks—"

"I got it," Jetta reassured me. She then stealthily lunged in my direction, quickly removing the ballpoint pen I'd wrapped in my hair.

Eric and I passed Alissa and Joe in the hallway, and Eric invited both of them to join us. While I understood, I didn't want him inviting anyone. I could tell Joe was about to accept when Alissa, who was already shaking her head, said, "That is so nice of you, but we've already eaten."

Joe turned to her with furrowed brows. "No, we—"

Alissa narrowed her eyes at her boyfriend while smiling. I interpreted this as a determined "Shut up!" She had obviously been talking to Jetta; that much was clear. Alissa looked a little pale, and I assumed this was because she was afraid Joe would end up accepting an invitation she clearly believed should not have been given.

"*Yes*, we have." Alissa turned to Eric and smiled again.

Joe cleared his throat. "Uh, she's right. We have already eaten. We ordered in—"

"Chinese. We had it delivered not too long ago. Right?"

Poor Joe. He was trying so hard to not ruin Alissa's plan even though it made no sense to him.

"Right. I don't know how I forgot. But thank you."

Eric gave a quick reply, and I looked to Alissa. "Hey, I'll bring those files you asked for as soon as I get back."

"Don't worry about it." She shook her head again. "Take all the time you need. *No rush*. I can come see you some time before leaving for the day." Alissa and Joe walked past us.

"Where would you like to go?" he asked when the elevator doors closed.

I thought for a few seconds. "Well, there's this little deli Jetta and I go to sometimes. They have great food, and it's within walking distance."

"Sounds good." There was that captivating grin again.

I did my best to ignore it, though. Had I allowed it, that grin would have easily pulled me into the fantasy world again. It was a world that consisted only of Eric and me.

Once I entered that world, I didn't want to leave. Standing next to Eric was so not the time to visit the fantasy again. To stop myself from daydreaming, I asked him how their project was going.

"I guess we've made a lot more progress by this point than we normally would. Things are moving really fast," he told me.

"That's great! I know Joe's team likes working with you and your team."

"Just not the twenty thousand meetings a week, right?" Eric said with a laughing sparkle in his eyes. "I doubt they love having their conference rooms filled up with bankers."

Well, I couldn't say he wasn't at least partially right. No one liked having a thousand meetings a week.

"Don't be silly! They appreciate how interested you guys are in the process."

He slid a glance my way as we stepped outside. "Come on. I know Mari. She tells you to say things like that, doesn't she?"

I couldn't help but laugh. Here was a man who saw things as they were and found humor in them. "Okay, the creative team doesn't like dressing up all the time. No one in the agency does, or at least none of the copywriters. But you really have been one of the agency's best clients. So involved, so cooperative. Not every overhaul goes as smoothly as yours has. We did an overhaul once that was still in the very beginning stages after six months."

I was unfortunately on that campaign, and all I could say was thank God I blocked out most of the details. I definitely did not want to relive that again. The entire process took so long it had me contemplating switching to an easier job, like electrical engineering.

Eric and I turned the corner, a few doors down from the deli. I squinted in the sunlight, which braved the afternoon after hiding behind clouds all morning. This was an early December day and slightly warmer than average. It was a huge difference from the previous three very chilly days. I found myself actually looking forward to the middle of winter just so the weather would make up its mind. I had never been a big fan of the temperature roller coaster that was autumn.

I told this to Eric, and he laughed at me. "Would you rather go back to the blistering heat of this past summer?"

"No, but that's what swimming pools and air conditioning are for." I slid a look at him. "Okay then, what season do you like most?"

He took a few seconds to answer. "Summer, I suppose."

"Even with all its blistering heat?"

"Yeah. Well, more the night than the day. A warm night with an ice-cold beer. I live in an old Victorian house, so I like to sit on the front porch swing most summer nights. I like watching thunderstorms pass nearby when I'm outside. Seeing the lightning flashing in the distance. It's pretty cool."

I instantly sucked in a breath of worry. "Isn't that dangerous?"

"I don't know," he shrugged. He was so casual about the way he moved. "I guess it could be, but it isn't like I'm out there when the storms are directly overhead. Usually. You know, I think it's something you might like to do."

"Sit on your porch watching thunderstorms roll by?"

"Sure. Why not?"

I didn't want to tell him how much I really hated thunderstorms.

"So, you spent your whole childhood in Evanston?" Eric ventured.

I nodded. "My parents live in the house my mom's parents' bought almost twenty years ago. It was the first house my grandparents owned in America after emigrating from Mexico."

"That's amazing."

"Yeah. I'm so proud of them for following their dreams. They've always encouraged me to follow mine as well. And actually, they still live in the same neighborhood, one street away from my folks. Despite how close they all are to me, I don't often get to see them."

"I know what you mean. My parents also live in the house I grew up in."

"Where is that?"

"Valparaiso."

I thought for a moment. "I'm assuming you don't mean in Chile."

"No," he laughed, "although that's the first thought that comes to people's minds. Valparaiso, or Valpo as we call it, is about thirty or so miles beyond the Indiana state line. I see my family on holidays. Sometimes, big family occasions like weddings or birthdays. That's about it. I feel bad about the distance, but it usually can't be helped."

We arrived at the deli after a few more steps. Even though we both reached for the handle at the same time, he grabbed it and held the door open for me. The place was quiet for early afternoon, a nice change from how boisterous the street had just been. Once inside, we ordered at the counter before finding an empty table. Only a handful of the other tables were taken, giving us plenty to choose from.

With all the options, Eric chose the best one, away from everyone else yet still with just the right amount of sunlight shining in from the window.

The deli had a distinct and permanent aroma of pastrami, mustard, and vinegar. It was always very clean but slightly faded. I liked to think of it not as old but well-used.

Once I noticed that my companion had already removed his outer coat, I did the same, revealing my modernist floral-printed midi dress in similarly-hued shades to my scarf. Eric glanced at my dress and smiled. If I was Jetta, I would have checked to see if he looked at my breasts. I could almost hear Jetta's voice in my head telling me to move my scarf and make my chest visible for Eric's viewing pleasure. I ignored this thought and put my coat on the booth seat next to me.

After our food was brought over, our conversation began to turn to our favorite things.

"Movie?" I asked.

"Easy," he smiled. "*The Blues Brothers*."

I cast a sideways glance to him. "You're kidding, right?"

"What? It's a good movie!" he exclaimed as he opened a tiny parcel of freshly-made potato chips. His deep, friendly voice echoed in the tiny deli, straight through my ears and into my memory. "It's got everything: comedy, action, great music."

I must have made a face because he added, "Have you ever watched it before?"

I thought a moment. Did I ever see it? "Not the whole thing. Bits and pieces, mostly. It's the one with John Belushi, right?"

Eric quietly stared at me for a few seconds, an unreadable expression in his eyes. "Do you talk through movies?"

"I try not to, but it still happens especially when I'm confused or I don't have the patience to wait for what's going to happen. That might be a reason why I've never seen that entire film."

"You should watch it with me. I'll explain to you what's going on, and you can ask whatever questions you want. Through the first viewing, anyway. I can't guarantee that every other time."

My stomach flipped itself into a knot. "Yeah." I grinned in return, my breath uneven and my face hot. "We should watch it together. That would be great."

I realized that Eric and I made a lot of "we should" plans but, as of yet, hadn't followed through on them. I desperately wanted us to keep those plans. I wanted to go on a hayride and search for constellations with him. I wanted him to show me what was so great about his favorite movie. I was even a little excited at the prospect of watching a thunderstorm with him—from a very safe distance, of course. And maybe for only five or so minutes. I wondered if Eric felt the same as me.

"I like a lot of ice cream flavors," Eric answered as I continued questioning him. "Vanilla, strawberry, cheesecake, cookie dough. I always have ice cream in the house in whatever part of the freezer that doesn't contain pizza."

This gave me a perfect glimpse into Eric's bachelor lifestyle. Pizza, ice cream, beer, good friends, and movies that no one talked through.

"Sounds like you have as big a sweet tooth as I do." I leaned forward a little in order to whisper. "I'm a bit of a chocoholic." I leaned back again and lifted my sandwich in anticipation of my next bite. "Color?"

Eric shook his head silently in reply.

"Oh, come on! You have to have a favorite color. Everyone has a favorite color."

"I don't know. I guess whatever looks good on a car."

I nearly choked on my carbonated drink. Some of it shot up into my nose, causing a burning, tear-inducing sensation. I coughed a few times, then replied, "So, which ones are acceptable?"

"Well, there's red and black. Sometimes gray. Occasionally silver. White, so long as you don't mind it being filthy all the time."

"You just named four shades and one color."

"What can I say? It's the only thing I'm picky about. That and mushrooms."

"So, we've established your least favorite food?"

"Definitely." He nodded, cringing.

We shared more back-and-forth questions and answers for the rest of our meal. It was so fun. So. Much. Fun. I laughed and smiled more with him than I ever knew was possible.

Once we finished lunch, Eric handed a tip to the waiter, then offered to join me on the return walk to my building. The reasonable side of my brain told me he offered merely because that was where he had left his car. This didn't stop me from being flattered. Or from grinning stupidly during the first few minutes back.

"How did you meet Logan?" Eric hesitated. "I haven't asked you that yet, have I?"

"Not yet." I smiled. "Logan and I have known each other since middle school. We were in the same grade but didn't hang out with the same people. We reconnected two years ago. He was with a friend. I was with Stephanie. We bumped into each other at the movies. We all decided to hang out somewhere after we watched the movie together. Logan and I became good friends from then on. We sort of fell into dating by accident."

Eric's brows crinkled. "How so?"

"Well, all of our friends were coupled at the time. Logan and I were the only single ones. Every party, every get-together. So, we just pretended we were a couple. It began as a joke. One day, Logan and I started making kissy faces to each other and calling each other the most absurd, sickeningly sweet pet names we could think of."

"Such as?" Eric asked with a curious look.

"Well, like Gumdrop, Sugarplum, and Little Lovey-Bug. Baby-Waby Cuddle Bear was my favorite."

Eric and I worked our way through a crowd of people in order to reach the crosswalk. I continued. "We carried on in this way for, oh, a good month, I'd say. Then we realized that we weren't pretending anymore. With the cuddles, kissy faces, and everything else, we'd somehow become a real couple."

I paused in my words as Eric and I walked. I realized Logan and I must have sounded pretty dull. That or crazy.

I shrugged to Eric. "It's a lame story, I know."

"No, it isn't. I find it interesting." He smiled. "I've never heard of anyone starting a relationship that way."

"I'm sure you never will again." Then I added, "You know, I honestly like Logan better as my boyfriend."

There was an expression on Eric's face that I couldn't quite read. "Why is that?"

"I get to see the kinder side of him that our friends don't see." As I spoke, I became aware of how different those words sounded aloud than in my head. "Not that he's a bad friend. He's not. He's always there for his friends when they need him. He loves spending time with his friends and doing what he can for them. They're very high on his priority list."

"Okay," Eric replied with a complaisant smile.

Crap. I'd found myself feeling the need to defend Logan yet again. Where that had come from, I had no idea. Was I so insecure about my relationship that I had to make Logan look good to everyone?

My phone dinged. I realized I'd forgotten to silence it when Eric and I left my office. I tried to ignore it, but he spoke up.

"Aren't you going to check that? It could be important."

My chest tightened at the thought of it being Mari. I pulled the phone out and looked at the screen.

Jetta: How is it going?

Me: Problems with Mari?

Jetta: Nope. All good here.

I didn't send a return message. I simply shoved my phone into my coat pocket and adjusted my scarf. Since Eric and I covered our favorites in the deli, I decided to ask him if there was anything besides mushrooms that he didn't like, starting with anything about himself.

He quickly cast a sideways glance at me. "Don't tell me there's something you don't like about yourself, Christabel."

"Well," I began, nervous about telling him the truth, "if I could change anything, it would probably be my hips." I looked over and caught him frowning.

His heart-melting eyes never left my face. "They look pretty perfect to me."

I felt the heat profusely burning my cheeks at this. "I've always been self-conscious of them. I suppose it doesn't help that my grandma used to tell me that I have child-bearing hips."

"Those hips would be perfect for having my children."

Our footsteps immediately halted. We looked at each other. His face was flushed to about as deep a red as mine felt.

"Um, what was that?" I asked at the same time he said, "I'm so sorry." We chuckled in the awkwardness.

He held his hands up. "I'm sorry," he said again. "It came out wrong. I didn't mean it the way it sounded. I just meant that I assume my kids will be big babies because I was."

"You were a big baby?" I slowly repeated.

"Yes. Huge. Well over eleven pounds. And I just—" He sighed, removing his glasses for a moment to rub his face with his hands.

"It's okay," I put a hand up to him. "I understand what you meant." That didn't stop my heart from fluttering. He was the first man who ever even pseudo-insinuated he wanted me to have his children. I really didn't know what to do with that.

Apparently, neither did Eric. He at least tried to shift the subject a little. While still not moving, he asked, "Do you want that in the future? The whole marriage and/or kids thing?"

"Sure. Someday. I mean, I was definitely one of those little girls who dreamed of her wedding day." The little girl who had five different wedding gowns for Barbie because one simply was not enough. The girl who put a pillowcase on her head as a veil and had weddings with her dolls and stuffed bears as guests. The girl who, when allowed, would try on her mother's fanciest dresses and pretend every one of them was a bridal gown. Not that Eric needed to know any of that yet.

We both began to smile, and I forced myself to glance away. "But that's not something I'm worried about right now. I am so not ready for settling down."

"But you still want your own family one day?"

I slowly nodded, tucking a few stray hairs behind my ear. "It would depend, though. There are a lot of factors to think about. And the fear that comes with the thoughts of raising a child. But the idea of having children is nice. You?"

He laughed, his eyes crinkling a little behind his glasses. "Eventually, yeah, but I think I need to focus on getting the girl first."

"Yeah, that's probably a good idea." Though I smiled, the idea of Eric being with another woman made my knees buckle in panic.

"Do you see that kind of future with Logan?"

Eric had no idea how loaded that question was.

Despite not believing I knew how to fall in love, I often saw a future with one certain man. I just didn't know who he was. He was literally my dream man.

There was one recurring dream in particular that stuck in my mind. I was all dressed up, dancing with the faceless man to a beautiful soundtrack of romantic music. The man held me close, whispered in my ear, and kissed me softly. I could touch him, smell him, and hear his heartbeats. There was a distinct feeling of being excited yet also comfortable with him. Being with him felt like being home.

But no matter how hard I tried, I couldn't distinguish his facial features. My mind wouldn't show me anything above his shoulders. Who was this man with no face?

"I have no idea," I unintentionally blurted.

Eric and I stared at each other again in another round of awkwardness. It was obvious he wanted to say something but held back.

He cleared his throat and tugged at his dark green tie. I, meanwhile, fidgeted with a pleat in my knee-length skirt. It was best for us to just start walking again. We passed a woman in her early thirties easily maneuvering a stroller down the sidewalk that contained the most adorable baby boy.

So not funny, I thought, looking up to the sky.

As Eric and I continued on, we were silent. Our easy banter had been replaced by hushed contemplation. On the plus side, we'd learned a lot about each other in that hour.

Eventually, we reached my lobby, where he left me to head for his car. I waved and smiled at him before walking to the stairs. A major part of me wished he could have walked me all the way up.

On my floor, three flights of stairs later, I slowly made my way to my desk, where I found Jetta waiting for me. She had been leaning against the desk but stood up with excitement once I was closer.

"It was a nice lunch," I slowly told her, walking around behind the desk to set down my coat and purse.

"Like how nice? Getting flowers nice?"

"When did you become so obsessed with someone sending me flowers?"

"I don't know. I figure it's bound to happen eventually simply based on the fact that you never get any sent to you."

"Do you get flowers every single time you have sex with someone?"

She motioned to the full vase that sat atop her desk.

"My goodness," I said. "You could have saved them all some money and invested in a greenhouse or something."

Jetta grinned and silently nodded in agreement.

"Anyway, it was nearly more than just Eric and me. We ran into Joe and Alissa before we left. Eric asked them to join us, but Alissa said no before Joe could even open his mouth."

"Oh, did she?" Jetta asked innocently.

"Mm-hmm. Like she knew there was a particular reason they needed to refuse the invite. What exactly have you been telling her?"

"I might have mentioned something about Eric. I don't remember any specifics, though."

"Uh-huh. Well, you didn't need to bother. Eric's a friend. That's all." I turned away before Jetta could read my face. To hide what I was really feeling, I slowly began removing my scarf.

My phone trilled with the sound of a new text.

Eric: Thanks for a great day.

Oh, Eric.

Though the corners of my mouth immediately began to curve up, I willed them to stay right where they were. I casually closed out the text and set my phone down on my desk, my heart thumping loudly in my ears the whole time.

Okay, okay. This was bad. I was in a precarious position. How could I admit my feelings for Eric? How was I supposed to say that, yes, everything he did made me like him more? Logan would never forgive me.

"Friend?" Jetta asked in surprise as I turned to face her.

I had collected myself enough to look at her and not give my thoughts away. "Yes. Friend. I have Logan, remember?"

"I know, I know. Have they met?"

"Several times. They're friendly. Most of the time. Eric often has an odd expression on his face when I'm around."

"So, these interactions with Eric could possibly turn into more than just friendly lunches."

"No." I shook my head at her.

"*Yes. They. Could.*" She paused, watching me. I saw a mischievous sparkle glow in her eyes. "I've got it. You should date them both."

I sent her an eye-roll. "I don't think my boyfriend would appreciate that."

"As long as you don't screw Eric—though I don't know how you couldn't—why would Logan care? You already said knowing about the lunch wouldn't bother him."

"Because dating someone is different than sharing a meal with them."

"Yeah, except you and Logan haven't made any commitments."

"I am not interested in Eric," I told her while avoiding eye contact.

"So, you're just straight-up lying to me now? Is that what's happening here?"

Yes. "No."

Her silence told me she didn't believe me.

"*If* I am attracted to him—"

"*If*? Seriously?"

I ignored her and continued. "I have no right to be."

"Why not?"

Tears began to well in my eyes. "Jetta- I—" I took a deep breath. "I've never cheated on anyone. Ever. Never had feelings for someone else while in a relationship. I just can't. It isn't... I just can't."

From the corner of my eye, I saw her nod as if she understood. Then she spoke again. "Eric's single."

"Yes, but—"

"Are you honestly going to tell me that you don't think of Eric during the course of a day? Really? You don't wonder where he is and what he's doing? You don't pay attention to the days he has meetings in our building?"

"Well, I—"

"You don't ever wonder if Eric is thinking about you, too?"

I finally looked my best friend in the eyes. I had no answer for her, and she knew why.

"Chrissie, don't you get it? The only reason you won't admit to liking Eric—other than some inane rule our company has—is a stupid sense of loyalty and obligation you feel for your jackass of a boyfriend."

Damn. Why did she have to know me so well? I chose to lie, anyway.

"Jetta, you have no idea what the reality of the situation is."

"I understand the dynamics of the situation perfectly. I also know what I've witnessed. You have to have noticed the way Eric looks at you. I'm sure I'm not the only one who's seen it. It's so obvious. His whole face lights up when he sees you. Didn't you notice how happy he was when you said you'd join him for lunch?"

"Yes, but that was probably because he didn't want to go back to his office so soon. I helped him avoid work."

"It was about so much more than that. I see it every time he's around you. He wants you. It shows on his face and in his eyes. You are the *only* one he wants to pay attention to, look at, and be around."

I'd had enough. "Jetta, that is such a load of sh—" I stopped.

She raised her eyebrows to me. "Of...?"

"Sh-sharply decided crap."

"Uh-huh. Right. Well, you're wrong. I know I would love for someone like Eric to want me the way he wants you. I think Eric is a good guy."

I nodded with a smile. "Yeah. He is." Lowering myself to my chair, I paused a moment, realizing what had escaped me earlier. "I didn't think much of this when it happened, but I noticed that Eric always took the side of the walkway closer to the road both to and from the deli. He also did that on our walk during the first baseball party. I was always closer to the buildings than the streets."

Jetta leaned against my desk again before pulling herself up to a sitting position on top of it. "Did he do it on purpose?"

I shrugged, remembering how casually he'd stepped to my other side each time. "Maybe."

"So, not only is he sweet, sexy, and intelligent, he's also caring and protective. He sounds like the perfect guy."

He did sound like the perfect guy. When I spoke again, my voice was much softer.

"Loretta told me that Eric once spent his whole vacation week helping a friend finish working on their house. I guess that guy's family needed to move into the house before being forced into signing another lease on their temporary apartment. Eric never even complained about the trip he gave up in order to help them. He said it was no big deal because they needed him. I guess he does stuff like that all the time."

"Hmm."

"What?" I looked up at her.

"If I wasn't so sure of his attachment to you, I think I might want him for myself."

I hated the idea of Jetta and Eric together. I absolutely loathed it. It made me feel physically ill. "Jetta, please don't say things like that again."

The expression on her face told me she was sorry and that she'd also accomplished what she set out to do. She spoke again, softer this time. "Someone has taken over your mind again, hasn't he?"

I opened my mouth to deny it, but I knew it was no use.

Jetta gave me a small, compassionate smile, jumping to her feet. "I'll leave you to your thoughts."

Chapter Twelve

I wasn't sure what my thoughts were on the subject. All I knew was that I couldn't allow a certain man to invade my mind. I had important work to do.

I looked at the stack of papers on my desk, deciding to concentrate on them right away. As I glanced at the pages returned from my CD a few days before, I re-read several remarks of hers about how she loved my streamlined idea and thought it needed only a few more tweaks. High praise from Mari for sure. I nearly fell out of my chair at the sight of her words.

The concept was a blend of ideas developed by Robert and me. Our pitches to Mari had been remarkably similar, so it naturally made sense to combine the two.

Well, it naturally made sense to me. Almost everyone else suggested letting Robert take over. It was because he was Mari's darling. No one else was willing to risk upsetting her by disagreeing with her. They were also unwilling to admit this.

I fought for my own concept long enough that Mari finally gave in with a huff and a roll of her eyes. I knew she agreed to let me stay on the campaign if only to stop me from finishing my thirty-point speech on why I deserved partial credit.

I didn't really think of thirty points, since I had all of two seconds to come up with them. I'd come up with eight and was interrupted on number seven.

The final pitch was rapidly approaching, which meant things had to be perfect as soon as possible. The perfect visuals, the perfect oral presentation, even the perfect attitude for such a meeting.

There was added pressure because Jetta had already been assigned to a new project, leaving Robert and me to figure something out together, and fast. Except he hadn't returned from lunch—a strange occurrence for him. He'd never missed a day or even half a day since I started at the agency. Ever.

Jetta suspected this absence was Robert's way of pressuring me, trying to prove how much I needed him in order to do anything.

"He wants you to fail," she told me as soon as she found out he went home, "but you won't give him the satisfaction. You are going to kick ass with or without him. You don't need him."

"That isn't entirely true. I do need him. Without Robert, I have our blended concept but nothing new he added to it in the last day or so. You and I both know he's been changing whatever he can to make it more his work than mine. Mari will insist on going with his ideas if I can't figure this out."

Jetta rubbed her cheek and bit her lip but offered no thoughts.

After considering the issue at hand, I said, "I have a plan."

"What's that?"

"Well, Robert would never do anything to help me, but he would do whatever it took to help himself."

"This is true. So, how's this going to go?" Her eyes sparkled. She was hoping for something devious, I knew.

"It's simple. I'll play on his love of rules and order. I'll tell him not sending everything he has to me right now will only hurt his job."

"That's the plan?" Jetta rolled her eyes. "You aren't even going to slip a veiled threat into it?"

"Well, I am going to put extra emphasis on him sending his files immediately. I mean, he should've told me he was leaving so I wouldn't wonder. He could have left the files here before disappearing. I'll also say that his not sharing will reflect negatively on him, not me. He will never get a promotion in this office if he suddenly falls from Mari's good graces."

Jetta smiled. "Now you're talking."

After sending Robert a quick, strongly-worded text and receiving a punctual reply, I knew I wouldn't see him again until our private meeting the next morning. He said he would email me all he had relating to the campaign, but he couldn't do much more. The threat worked, though it still couldn't bring Robert to the office. This left me by myself to figure out precisely what Mari, and in extension, Paolo and the client, wanted changed.

I kicked myself for not focusing on the project while Robert was still at work.

Apart from my job, I'd never been able to figure out what it was that people wanted from me. I didn't usually know what they were looking for. If I was ever lucky enough to understand, it was typically after a lot of time and a lot of wrong guesses.

Like with Logan. I didn't always understand what he desired. Well, sure, a few specific things I knew. Obviously. But not about what he wanted with me and with us. Were all his back and forth "I knows" just a passive-aggressive way of asking me to tell him what to do? If this was the case, would he honestly accept my suggestions?

Then again, if I was wrong and he didn't want me telling him what to do, any input from me would be unwelcome. At the very least, he'd think me bossy. He might say I had no right making decisions for him. How dare I take control of his life? That sort of thing.

I assumed it would turn out one of these ways, but would Logan ever tell me for sure?

It was all too much for me to understand. Then there was Eric. I had no clue about anything that he wanted. He preferred asking me about my life and goals instead of talking about his own.

Unfortunately, all this confusion about, well, everything basically, had seeped into my assignment. I thought I knew what needed to be done, but as I stared at the pages in front of me, I felt my confidence slipping away. I could not get my brain to understand Robert's notes. Then I began second-guessing every aspect of my ideas, every path I took with them. The more I read through my notes, the less sense they made. My anxiety ramped up its attack on me and shut down any critical thinking.

Happily, though, Jetta had generously offered to help give me a different perspective on the tweaks. We'd decided to meet up after work. Until then, I was on my own.

Reading through both my typed and hastily handwritten notes again, some aspects finally began falling into place. Not a lot of the components. Just enough that I could begin with them and go from there. Robert's meticulously crafted outline suddenly became comprehensible, though it still failed to spark any cohesive ideas at first. To help jumpstart my creativity, I typed whatever popped into my head. Any thought related to this project appeared, letter by letter. I was so focused on my computer screen that I jumped at the voice speaking beside me.

"Hey! You ready?"

I looked up at Jetta, momentarily confused. "Ready for what?"

"Work's over, Chrissie," she smiled, adjusting the zipper on her jacket. "Everyone else decided to take off. Time to go home."

"Is it really?" I rubbed my bleary eyes, then glanced at my watch. 8:47 PM. Another near fourteen-hour day. Not bad considering how soon the pitch was scheduled. Most days had an additional two or three hours on them at least.

"Uh, yeah. I'm ready. Let me just..." I printed out what I'd been working on, stuffing all the papers along with my "when I get ideas on the go" notebook into my bag, moving my laptop to one side in order to make room. I grabbed my scarf and coat and walked with Jetta to the elevator.

Once we were finally outside, we headed to my car in a nearby parking garage. A few minutes later, we stopped for food and drove to Jetta's place in the West Loop, not too far from the agency.

I loved Jetta's apartment. It was a loft, and it was huge compared to mine. It used to be a factory at one point before being converted into something more livable. Everything was sleek and modern yet still industrial. Concrete, exposed brick, steel beams, and the like. Despite the factory-like look of its structural bones, Jetta's apartment still managed to feel comfortable enough to be a home and chic enough to match her personality.

It was quite the opposite of my own apartment. Because of my rent agreement, I wasn't allowed to paint the walls anything more colorful than, well, oatmeal. Maybe oatmeal with a *bit* of light brown sugar. Since my only other option was white, I decided to decorate around my oatmeal walls, using various shades of deep, chocolate-y browns, rich caramels and soothing creams.

After we arrived, we had chipotle chicken burritos with black bean salsa and blue corn tortilla chips for dinner. Jetta gave me the scoop on Cute Neighbor Guy's newly single status.

"Again? Isn't that, like, his fourth breakup this month?"

"Third. And two were with the same woman."

I watched her for a moment, trying to gauge her feelings about this. Slowly, I asked, "Do you think you're next?"

She laughed. "Chrissie, *please*. We have totally moved on from that. Like, ages ago. Now we just platonically flirt. No feelings allowed."

"Friends that flirt?"

"Yep."

"Whatever works for you." I grinned.

"Oh, it does." She grinned back. Then she said, "Did I tell you what happened with that attorney I was dating?"

I thought if she hadn't told me about Carlos, she certainly hadn't told me about some lawyer. I looked over at her. "You were dating a lawyer?"

"I really wish we'd stayed friends."

Uh-oh. "Why do you say that?"

"Well, after one of our dates—the last one, in fact—we went to his place to have a couple drinks. After a while, it started getting hot in there, and—"

"You mean hot and heavy."

She grinned. "Anyway, as he pulled off his sweater, I saw how hairy he was."

"You stopped dating him because of some hair?"

"Not just some hair." She quickly shook her head. "A lot of it. I mean, it was like he still wore his sweater, even though it was on the floor next to us. He was completely covered in long, thick, curly body hair. There was just too much resemblance to a grizzly bear for me to stay. I told him I had a sudden headache, like migraine-style, grabbed my shoes, and high-tailed it out of there."

I couldn't hold in a snort. "Was it that bad?"

"Chrissie, I had nightmares that night of being attacked by a bear. As I was finally able to break free, I realized it was Danny following me." She shuddered, and I took another bite of burrito to keep from laughing.

We soon finished our dinner and began setting up our makeshift work station in the living room area. As I switched on my laptop, I noticed Jetta looking at me.

"What?" I asked, subconsciously running my tongue over my teeth to check for stubborn food pieces that had decided to stick around.

Silently, she chewed her lip, then started that hair twirling thing again.

I watched her, both of my hands on my computer, waiting for the login screen. She knew I was waiting for her to speak again. I hoped it would be a good question. An easy one, like, "What was your favorite color when you were three?" No relationship drama, no mysteries of the heart. *Please be my favorite color!*

Finally, she said slowly, "I was just wondering when the last time was that you saw Logan. You haven't mentioned him much lately. You only talk about him if I bring him up."

If I lied, would she believe me? Could I tell her the truth without it becoming a big deal? Honestly, I didn't have the answers to these questions.

I pulled up the program I needed as I shrugged and answered, "Early last week."

"But, Chrissie, it's already Thursday."

I avoided eye contact with my best friend.

Chapter Thirteen

My phone dinged with a new text message. I picked it up and silently read the words.

Eric: Lunch again next week?

My heart fluttered. I smiled, replied with a yes in a way I hoped didn't sound too ecstatic, and then shoved the phone back in my purse, hoping Jetta wouldn't ask me what that was all about.

"I know I haven't had any contact with Logan in a while." I sighed without meaning to.

"So, this must explain the ugly bracelets, huh?" Jetta asked.

I gave her a smile. "Sort of. But it's all right. No big deal. I hadn't thought much of not being able to see Logan until now. You know, except for why I'm wearing these stupid things." I glanced at my adorned wrist.

Jetta pulled a face. "I hope Eric didn't see those."

Me, too, I thought.

Jetta quickly returned to the original topic. "Why has it been so long since you've seen Logan? He lives ten minutes from you, not ten hours."

"I know. He's busy, though."

Jetta gave me a look. "What is he busy with?" She demanded more than asked this.

I decided to list things starting from the day after we were last together. "Work, basketball, guys' night, school project, school project, work, school project, work, guys' night, basketball, brutal headache. And he's at work tonight. On the plus side, Logan actually told me what he was busy doing this time. That is a huge breakthrough for him. Progress is always good in a relationship."

She shook her head. "Wasn't all this supposed to get better once the World Series ended? I thought that without the baseball distraction, he'd make an effort to spend more time with you."

"It did get better. Work and school are both very important to him, as they should be."

"Oh please. Are you in a 'Stepford Wives' training class or something?"

I let that comment slide. "It isn't like he can't go out with his friends whenever he wants."

"Going out with his friends is fine. He just seems to go out with them three times as much as he goes out with you, and you're his girlfriend."

"But he calls me more now than he ever has."

"When did he call you last?"

"He texted me last night before bed."

"A text is not the same as a phone call. You can't hear the person's voice in a text." She paused. "So, wait... that text you just got wasn't from Logan?"

I shook my head no.

"Hmm. You smiled like it was."

I gave no answer for this. What could I say? Instead, I steered the conversation back to Jetta's original topic. "It's okay that Logan hasn't called. I mean, I know what his voice sounds like. And we're seeing each other tomorrow."

"Are you ever going to stop making excuses for him?"

"I don't do that."

"Yes, you do."

"Okay, so what if I do? Mind you, those are genuine reasons why I haven't seen him, not lame excuses like I know you think they are."

"I never said that." Jetta gave a smirk.

"You didn't have to. Anyway, Logan and I are good right now. I think we're slowly finding our way to a happy medium."

"Well, you know what would make him a whole lot happier."

I gave no answer.

"I know it's been a long time since you've used birth control. If you haven't taken the pill before, know they are not that bad. I like mine." She paused. "On second thought, you might not be the right person to remember to take a pill every day."

Well, she was right about that one.

"It isn't about birth control." I gave a headshake. "I know all about the pill, IUDs, the ring, the patch, and everything else. That is not the issue."

She watched me. "Oh! Okay. I see. Has it just been too long since you've had sex? You don't need to be embarrassed. What he wants is actually the easy part. The harder stuff comes with mastering the art of seduction. You don't need to try too hard with that, though."

"Please, just stop. Now."

"I'm serious, Chrissie. It's nothing to be ashamed of. Just remember that you want to be sexy yet playful at the same time. The worst thing you can do is take it too seriously. You want it to be fun. And no matter what you try, don't bother with the tying a cherry stem in a knot thing. It is so not easy, and you could choke. I almost did once. Well, twice. Stick with the simpler things. What I always like to start with is—"

I put a hand up to stop her. "Jetta, seriously. *Please*. Me not sleeping with Logan has nothing to do with wanting something from him. Or not knowing how to seduce him."

I knew that I could be in the rattiest sweats I owned, my frizzy hair sticking up in places, and no makeup on my face, and Logan would still want to make love. If I asked him to, his mouth would be on mine before I even finished the question. No seduction necessary.

"He should be happy dating me, with or without that. Any of that."

"True. You are absolutely right. But does the idea of sleeping with him repulse you?"

I instantly had a mental image of Logan and me like that and tingled. "No. Of course not."

"Not even a little?"

Another tingle. "Not even a little."

"So, what's the problem? You say it isn't because of Eric. And you weren't having sex with Logan before Eric came along. You don't think having sex with your boyfriend would help anything? Even just a tiny, little bit?"

"It's a lot more complicated than physically wanting it. I think we have enough issues as it is without adding sex to the mix."

"Issues you refuse to talk to him, or anyone, about."

"*Anyway*," I said, ignoring her comment, "it isn't entirely Logan's fault. I'm sure there are things I've done or said that have hindered our relationship. I'm not perfect."

"We all know that's true."

I playfully smacked her with my closest hand. She laughed as she held her arm in pretend pain. "Besides, I work a lot. More than he ever does. Especially recently because of this pitch."

"On that note," Jetta said, pulling the coffee table closer to us, "what do you have to do?"

"Well, I have a really great headline. The body, the information, all that is perfect. I took a lot more from mine than Robert's, mainly because what I have makes more sense. It also relates more to the client's needs. I think it's my subhead that is bothering me. It doesn't matter whether I take it out or leave it in. Once I do one thing, I immediately feel the urge to do the other."

"I'm sure we can figure it out, Chrissie. No sweat."

As I moved the laptop from my knees to the table, I shook my head with a laugh. "You know, you're the only one who gets to call me that. I sure hope you appreciate it."

She smiled. "Oh, I do. It makes me feel special."

I took a brief second to gaze at my desktop picture. It was a fabulous one of Logan and me from that spring, just before we started dating.

About ten of us had been at a friend's duplex watching a movie we'd viewed a million times before. They all loved that movie; me, not so much. During one of the majorly boring parts which was, in fact, hilarious to the rest of them, I glanced outside and noticed it was snowing. March snow in our area is not uncommon, but I was so happy to see it that I threw on my boots and went outside. I didn't even take a coat.

I walked down to the yard and slowly turned around in circles, taking in the cold, beautiful moment. Logan followed soon after, two coats in hand. He handed me mine, then he put on his own. After he made sure my coat was buttoned up, we watched the snowfall together, full of smiles and laughter. Unbeknownst to us, while we watched the snow, Stephanie watched us and took the picture.

The program I was opening popped up, bringing me back to the present. I looked to Jetta again.

"Before we begin, would you like some wine?" she asked on her way to the kitchen.

"Sure. Thanks."

While waiting for Jetta, I organized my notes and previous presentations, as well as everything Robert emailed to me from his presentation.

After a minute or two, Jetta brought two glasses back from the kitchen, handing one to me. "Sparkling spritzers because the bubbles make it more fun."

Even regular wine was too boring for Jetta, and I loved that about her.

"Are you sure you can do this?" I asked as I finished perusing my notes.

"You deserve to see your own campaign through to the end. Robert and Mari had no right trying to take that away from you. Describe to me what you have so far, and we'll go from there."

We set to work, and by the end of an hour, we had the pitch absolutely perfected, subhead and all. I was honestly looking forward to my early meeting the next day.

The next day, once everything was agreed on and the meeting declared officially over, Mari stood and looked straight at me. "It's a good thing Robert saved you yesterday."

I felt like she'd sucker-punched me in front of everyone. So much for all the good energy I'd felt walking into the conference room an hour earlier. I didn't dare tell Mari that Jetta helped me. Lord knows Mari would have relished the fact that I needed someone else to work on the project with me.

Mari then waltzed out of the conference room with her phone to her ear, yelling at her assistant. Robert smirked at me before following behind her like a puppy. Paolo looked concerned but said nothing before walking away. Bruce, the art director, gave me a sad smile and left the room.

Natalia, the only other person in there, came over to me and put a hand on my arm in comfort.

Tears burned my eyes. "I'm not incompetent!" I told her in a hushed sort of scream.

"Of course, you're not. We all know that. What you just presented was far more your project than Robert's. You did great."

I angrily brushed at the tears, willing them to disappear so I could return to my desk. "Then why did Mari treat me like an idiot in front of you all, especially Bruce and Paolo? She completely humiliated me."

Natalia sighed. "You know how it is with her, Christabel. If Mari isn't happy, everyone's job is on the line. It makes no difference whether or not we work directly under her. Even Paolo and Bruce aren't completely safe. Just watch your back from now on, okay? I'd hate for you to lose your job."

"Wait. What do you mean?"

"I've been waiting for the chance to tell you this, but I overheard Mari and Paolo talking about you in the hall the other day. Mari said if you mess up this project with Robert, you'll be fired. Not him, just you. It all hinges on how you do."

"But that's not fair."

She shook her head. "No. It isn't. I wish I could do more to help you, but you and I both know Mari won't let anyone from the Art Department join you all other than in meetings."

I nodded. "I know. Thanks, Nat."

Now I really was concerned about my job.

Chapter Fourteen

Loretta and David actually got engaged during their trip to New York. The vacation was part of the proposal. I guess it was the surprise of all surprises—the pinnacle of the entire trip. They were throwing a casual engagement party at their house for all their friends and close family that Friday night.

Normally, Logan and I would have driven together, but we both worked late and had to meet there. We somehow arrived at approximately the same time. Once both cars were parked—not an easy task with several dozen other vehicles blocking the driveway and spilling out into the street—Logan and I greeted each other with a quick kiss and headed inside. The entire Cape Cod-style house and attached garage seemed filled to the brim with people, most of whom I didn't know. After dropping off our jackets in a guest bedroom, Logan and I had to weave our way through everyone to find the happy couple and congratulate them. They were surrounded by others but stepped away in order to greet us.

"How are you? It's so wonderful to see you!" Loretta told us.

David added with a smile, "Great to see you guys. Thanks for coming."

"Congratulations! We are so happy for you both!" I gushed in return.

We had just enough time for me to hug David and Loretta and give them a card before they were whisked away by new guests.

As Logan and I began to mingle, I found myself so happy to see the few people I knew but hadn't heard from in what felt like forever. We hugged, we talked, we laughed. I saw at least a dozen pictures of new babies and growing kids.

After a while, Logan and I found the buffet and mix-it-yourself bar in the crowded dining room. The bar was off to one side, while the buffet filled the whole dining table. It had a huge selection of meats, pastas, and snacks.

I selected a few nibbles of food. I wasn't particularly hungry. Mari had my stomach tied in knots after the morning meeting. Logan didn't waste any time heading straight for the alcohol. He grabbed a bottle of beer and chugged it down completely before opening a second and taking a huge swig, tipping the bottle up high to pour liquid down his throat.

"Are you all right?" I asked in a hushed voice, conscious of others near us. He drank the beer so easily that if I didn't know better, I would have sworn it was something he did on a regular basis. To be honest, though, I wasn't sure I did know better. Jetta's words began echoing in my brain. *"Who knows what he's doing without you? Do you?"*

"I'm fine." He smiled before taking another long swig. He finally removed the bottle from his mouth. "Why do you ask?"

Through my surprise, I stammered out an answer. "I've just never seen you down a beer like that before. I didn't even know you could."

He shrugged, but, to me, it was more like he was shrugging off my concern. "Yeah, I know. I had a hard day. Don't want to talk about it."

I had a difficult time not spouting off the more than fifty questions swirling in my head. Instead, I only let one out. "Are you sure you don't want to talk about it?"

He gave me a hard look with darkened, narrowed eyes.

Yep. He was sure. No words necessary.

Should I have changed topics? Absolutely.

Did I?

Hell, no.

"You're drinking a lot," I whispered to him.

"So what?" Logan asked, calmly reaching for his third beer.

"So, it's a lot for you. For being here all of twenty minutes. You should eat first. Here. Take some of these." I moved my appetizer-filled hand toward him, but he brushed it away.

"It isn't that much, Christabel. It also isn't a big deal."

"But you have your car here."

"Okay." He looked at me blankly.

I despised that look of his. It was an unsettling stare—one that made me feel stupid for having just said whatever it was that came out of my mouth.

I watched a few people leave the room before turning to Logan once more. "Okay, so that means you have to drive home again."

"I know that. I can take care of myself." He quickly finished off the rest of beer number three.

"You know that I'm not going to let you drive like this, right?"

"I do," he replied. His tone was relaxed.

Mine was not. "Do you also know that Loretta's grandparents are here, as is her aunt, who drove up from Kentucky just for this party?"

This was one of those moments when my brain screamed, "Shut up! *Shut up!*" However, my mouth refused to listen. My heart, well... it stayed out of the conversation entirely.

I pushed a little more. "You know this is an important party for them. It's to celebrate their engagement. Nothing should ruin that."

"Yes, I know," he answered slowly. "I'll behave myself. No stupid stunts. Don't worry." He kissed me quickly, tasting and reeking of beer. After setting the now-empty third bottle onto a nearby table, he smiled and said, "Let's go find Jesse."

Logan took my free hand as I held my napkin full of uneaten food in the other, and we left in search of our friend. I honestly put a lot of effort into looking for Jesse because I had no desire to wonder anymore about what had just transpired. I couldn't give in to all my questions in a house crammed full with other people.

We soon located Jesse in the living room, along with a few other guys Logan had been hoping to see. They were all on the same basketball team as David and wanted to discuss strategies for the next several games. I quietly munched on my hors d'oeuvres as the men talked on about critical defensive plays, changing the starting point guard, and so on. Really boring stuff, at least to me.

Since I wasn't included in their conversation, I glanced around the room to see what I might be missing. I quickly caught eyes with Eric, who must have arrived not long before. He looked happy to see me but also pained. *Deeply* pained.

For the first time, I fully realized what Jetta had been going on and on about. It was as clear as anything had ever been.

Eric's eyes had a distinct characteristic of adjusting their brightness to his happiness. The more ecstatic he was, the brighter and more vibrantly his eyes shone. In that moment, his eyes were as dark as I'd ever seen them. I saw passion, heartbreak, and confusion in them. I saw a man who wanted nothing more than to come to me but didn't dare.

Eric glanced to my immediate right. I self-consciously remembered that Logan stood there with his arm snugly around my waist. That seemed to hurt Eric more than anything. He gave me a small wave and walked away, disappearing into the sea of people.

I, meanwhile, no longer had an appetite. My stomach churned as much as my mind. I offered my last stuffed mushroom to Logan, who took it happily. He and Jesse stepped away to talk to David. In the mass of people, I somehow lost sight of them.

After a quick stop in the dining room to toss my napkin, I began to wander around the house, rejoicing in quiet corners and nearly empty rooms. Those were the only places I could reasonably contemplate what to do about the whole Eric thing without being interrupted by someone.

I was in one of the nearly empty rooms when Eric found me. While my back leaned against a wall, I'd half-wished I could go home until that moment, when he stepped next to me with a "hello."

"Hi." I smiled, my heartbeats steadily increasing.

"How are you?" His eyes scanned the room but soon focused on me.

"I'm well." I smiled again. I thought it best to limit eye contact for the moment while also showing him that he had my full attention. It was a delicate balance I wasn't quite sure I mastered. "You?"

"I'm pretty good, too."

"So, that's great about David and Loretta, huh?"

"Yeah. Not so unexpected. They're good for each other."

"Oh, yes. It wasn't a surprise, but it was certainly nice to hear."

We both sounded like robots. It was excruciating.

"A lot of people are here," Eric commented.

And one, in particular, neither of us was sure we wanted there.

"Did you come here straight from work?" I asked.

"Yep. *Long* day." He rubbed his face for a second or two, as if to wipe away his memories of the day.

"Same here. I thought I would never get out of the office."

He nodded, then glanced at the glass of water in my hand. During my wandering, I'd stopped in the kitchen for a drink. All the serious thinking, mixed with party-mingling, had made me super thirsty. "Not drinking tonight?"

I shrugged. "I'm not much of a drinker. Have to drive home tonight."

"That doesn't seem to be much of a concern for your boyfriend. Saw his car parked out front."

I gave an incoherent, mumbled answer in return.

Things were feeling different between us, and I didn't know if it was good or bad. I was sure he knew his secret was out, but I didn't know if he was going to do anything about it.

From the other room, we could hear Logan's now-drunken voice stupidly bellow out, "I'll bet you ten bucks I can drink that faster than you. I'll even do it upside down."

"You're on, man! No *way* you can do it," another drunken voice—Jesse, I assumed—replied.

I groaned and rolled my eyes. So much for behaving himself. Logan always loved idiotic dares.

I slowly moved my eyes to Eric, who grimaced as well.

After another second or two, he moved his body in front of mine, standing as close as he could without raising suspicions in the few strangers who were exiting the room, leaving us alone. He carefully took the water glass from my hand and set it on the floor by my feet. Another barrier between us removed. Once he straightened, he rested his left hand on the wall behind my head, leaving the top of him closer than the rest.

Eric was so close, in fact, that I could practically count each hair in his goatee. I could even smell the faintest hint of soda on his breath. I didn't know if it was cologne, body wash, or what, but he smelled clean and spicy and absolutely irresistible.

I began playing with the bottom hem of my blouse to avoid running my hands all over and under Eric's shirt. Though his jacket and tie were missing, he still wore a dress shirt, collar unbuttoned and sleeves rolled the way I like. Seeing Eric this way made my knees weak enough that I needed to lean more of my weight against the wall.

Being so near to him felt heady and intoxicating. As wrong as it was, I wanted to pull him to me. I wanted to feel his touch. I wanted to forget about everything and everyone else. While Logan was drunk on alcohol, I was becoming drunk on Eric.

With a lowered voice, Eric asked, "Christabel, what is it exactly that you see in Logan?"

"He does have a lot of good qualities. He isn't usually like this. He had an awful day today, which I think has clouded his mind a bit. He's usually a lot better than this."

While I knew it was true, in the moment, I couldn't actually think of Logan's good traits.. Not when his voice echoed out from next door, more intoxicated than I was used to seeing, his loud obnoxiousness drowning out everything I'd ever liked about him.

From Eric's face, I could tell he was listening, too. I could also tell that my previous answer wasn't good enough. "Why are you with him?"

I shook my head. "I don't know."

Eric looked at me with raised brows and wide eyes. "You don't know?" he asked, as if attempting to decipher my meaning.

I shook my head again. "No. Yes. I mean, I don't know how to tell you. I don't know what to say to make you understand."

"You can't even try?" There was a sort of desperation in his voice, his eyes, his everything. I had never seen a man so vulnerable before. He was pleading for something I wasn't sure I could give.

All that silent contemplation had definitely not prepared me for this. I'd expected him to talk about *us*. For whatever reason, I never thought he would ask me about Logan. "Eric, please. I can't explain it."

I looked earnestly in his eyes, trying to avoid the precise thing I was afraid of.

I wanted to release the tension that had built up. I wanted to make a joke. But I couldn't do it. Not now. Eric wanted serious answers for serious questions. I could tell the Q & A was not over yet. There was something he was holding back, something he was debating if he should let out.

This was the now or never moment. Would it all come down to an ultimatum? What would I do if it did?

He silently stared at me for a few almost never-ending seconds. The expression on his face was so solemn, it made me more than a little nervous. Finally, he spoke. "Do you love Logan?"

I sucked in a breath at his words. "Please don't ask me that."

Eyebrows furrowed, Eric tilted his head. "Why not? It's a fair question."

"No. No, it really isn't."

"You don't think so?"

I closed my eyes for a few seconds. "No. And I don't have an answer for that one, either. But I do care about him, and I know he cares about me." Probably. "You just don't understand."

Eric thought about that for a moment. Despite all the complications, he did the one thing I could always count on from him. He kept his eyes locked on me. And those poor eyes. They had given away his pain before, but now they revealed pure agony.

He moved even closer, a mere inch or so away from my body. Eric was so close, I couldn't fiddle with my hem anymore. My hands were unoccupied—a dangerous situation, indeed. He tentatively rested his free hand on my waist, just above my "perfect" hip. To my surprise, his touch made me feel more at ease than anything, even with his slight trembling.

"You're right. I don't understand. I don't get why you want to be with someone who ignores you all the time."

"Logan doesn't ignore me. Not all the time. Maybe once in a great while. A *great* while. Hardly ever." I couldn't believe it. I was defending my crappy relationship with one man while the heat of another man's hand was rushing into my side, warming everything else.

What in the world was happening? What was I doing?

"From what I can tell, it is most of the time." Eric's eyes added to the emphasis in his voice.

"Not entirely. I wouldn't call it 'ignoring' me, anyway."

I did not want to discuss Logan anymore. I wanted us to move beyond the subject of Logan into better subjects for a better conversation. Then, in a moment of weakness, I began playing with one of Eric's shirt buttons.

He gave me the tiniest of smiles before becoming serious again. "You cannot let your loyalty for your boyfriend outweigh all reason. You're clouding your judgement over a guy who doesn't deserve it."

Instead of answering, I fidgeted with Eric's buttons a bit more. I unbuttoned then re-buttoned the one I'd held on to and also one just above it. It wasn't easy, considering how close we were. My hands almost felt sandwiched between Eric's chest and my own. Warmth was radiating into me from more than just his hand.

How was it that we were so close to each other, especially in the physical sense, yet we had somehow found ourselves arguing about a man neither of us wanted to think of?

Eric shook his head in frustration. "He should have realized you were gone the night we took a walk. He should have noticed before Loretta said something. I would have."

My eyes darted up. "Eric—"

"For all Logan knew, you could have vanished at that party. He hadn't paid any attention to you, even before we left. For several hours before then."

"Well, that's not exactly true—"

"I guess it doesn't really matter," Eric sighed, stepping back from me and glancing away. The distance forced me to drop my hands, leaving them unoccupied once again. Though I wanted to reach out to him, I promptly flattened my palms against the wall behind me.

"What do you mean?" I whispered.

My body instantly felt cold when Eric let go. However, there was another kind of coldness that occurred, which had nothing to do with physical warmth. I looked in his face and didn't like what I saw. I had a sinking feeling I also wasn't going to like what came out of his mouth next, either.

"Christabel, I don't understand why you want Logan, but it's your choice. You picked him before I ever came along. And I'm going to let you live your life with him. You don't seem to mind Logan's shitty treatment of you. Who am I to say things have to change? I've been making myself crazy thinking about this, and I know it's the only thing I can do. I won't bother you anymore. At all." He let out a sigh, taking another long look in my eyes.

There was so much anguish in his face. His hurt was palpable to me. It was a crushing pain that took my breath away.

He stepped closer again, as if about to kiss me, but stopped short. And, oh, I didn't want him to stop. I wanted him to come all the way to me. I wanted him to wrap his arms around me and tell me everything was going to be okay so I wouldn't feel conflicted or confused anymore. I wanted to live out every fantasy I'd ever had about him.

I imagined Eric's lips brushing against my neck and his hand stroking my thigh. His hard body pressing into me. Things were getting so warm, I could hardly slow my quickening breath. Only this time, I wasn't red-faced or giggling. The thought of us like that didn't make me nervous at all. And I knew if I told him, he'd want the same thing, too. The kissing, the caressing, the passionate love-making.

But Eric wouldn't do anything about it. I knew he wouldn't. And deep inside, I didn't really want him to. *Mostly.* As much as we wanted to pretend differently, Logan was still my boyfriend.

I desperately wanted to ease the tortured expression on Eric's face. I swallowed hard as he moved in closer and opened his mouth. His voice was soft and empty against my ear. "Goodbye, Christabel."

Chapter Fifteen

The urge to cry almost overwhelmed me once Eric was gone. My breath emptied from my lungs, refusing to return to an almost crushing degree. I frantically tried to blink away hot moisture as my eyes burned. *I can't cry. I cannot cry*, I silently repeated to myself.

Despite my determination, little tear pools began flooding my eyes, blurring my vision.

If Eric hadn't taken my glass from me, it would have been on the floor by this point. Likely as shattered as I felt. I was shaking so much that I was sure nothing could steady me, not even the wall I still leaned against. My legs might as well have been broken. Eric flashed through my mind again, and my heart ached.

I didn't say goodbye to him. I was too shocked to form words. Even if I could have formed words, I had no idea what they would have been. Echoing his last sentiments would have broken my heart—that much I knew. Anything else would have sounded hollow or fake.

Anything except what I really wanted to say.

But I couldn't do it. I had no right to ask him not to leave me. I wasn't his to leave, anyway. He had been my friend at most, my company's client at the very least, neither of which afforded me the selfish luxury of asking him to deal with the pain of seeing me with Logan so long as I got to keep Eric close to me.

Everything felt surreal, almost like a dream world. No dreams I ever had about Eric ended like this, however. It was so awful, so painful. The only comfort I had was that I was finally alone in a room.

Truthfully, the last person I wanted to see was the next person to find me.

"There's my beautiful girl!" Logan exclaimed with a drunken grin, bursting into the quiet space. His moods had been changing faster than mine during PMS. It was hard to tell where this new happiness came from. Was it because of me, the booze, or something else?

After walking over to me, he leaned into me the way Eric had, only much, much closer. There were zero gaps between his body and mine. His hand was even exactly where Eric's had been on the wall.

"Hey, babe," he whispered into my ear.

"Hey, Logan." I forced a small smile.

I didn't think he would notice a little unhappiness. Even if he did, I always had that reliable backup of blaming it on work. This excuse was more apt to be believed by Logan than by anyone else. But would I need to use it?

"I missed you." He grinned again.

I couldn't say the same, so I said nothing at all. I also thought it best to limit eye contact. I couldn't hide the redness or puffiness of my eyes, but I thought it possible that

Logan would overlook those obvious signs of crying. He had been known to before.

But Logan wiped away one rebellious tear that had quickly escaped from my eye and was running down my cheek. "Are you all right?" he whispered.

So he did notice. I was a little relieved to be wrong.

"I'm okay. I think all the stress of my project finally caught up with me."

"You sure?"

I nodded.

"Okay. I'm sorry work has you so tense."

"Thanks." I faked a grin.

He gently brushed a few stray hairs away from my face then slowly stroked his thumb along my cheekbone. His hand was hot on my skin, making me realize I was chilly. Even colder than I was when Eric stepped away from me. Logan kissed my lips, more softly than he had in a long time.

We kissed for several seconds before he pulled back, smiling at me once more. "You know, I've been looking for you," he told me, pulling away from the wall, separating our bodies a little.

Yet another example of Logan's vagueness. How long had he been trying to find me? Where exactly had he looked?

"Well, I'm right here."

"Yes, you are. I'm so glad I found you." Something in his voice hinted that he meant it, that his happiness with me was about more than this instance. He pulled my body completely into his, squeezing me tight.

I relaxed into him despite myself. He was, after all, still my boyfriend. I also desperately needed a hug at that moment. And no one hugged like Logan. It was an entirely different experience with him than with anyone else. His hugs were firm and tender and comforting. Hugs were some of the best things he ever gave me.

"Come on." Logan stepped back. "We're missing the party."

I grabbed my glass off the floor and slipped my free hand into his. I was surprised that while he asked why I was upset, he never asked why my drink was on the floor. I suppose his brain was too busy trying to keep him on his feet for that to register. Walking required much more effort than standing, and he struggled to do both.

We walked down to the finished basement, where the remaining party guests had gathered in the large game room. More time had passed than I'd realized because there weren't many people left in the house. Most everyone was by the pool table, except for Loretta, who was busy playing darts with someone I didn't recognize.

Logan was wasted beyond what I thought him capable of. After I helped him down the stairs and through the small living area, I guided him into a chair near the less populated side of the game room. I was about to find a chair of my own when he deftly pulled me onto his lap and wrapped his arms around my stomach.

"Will you stay with me?" he asked quietly.

There was a vulnerability to the way he asked which made me wonder how he was feeling. I didn't think that I would receive an answer if I asked. I needed to find out some other way.

I turned to face him and noticed just how foggy his eyes looked. I had no idea what Logan drank, but the fact that he smelled like a distillery, even from ten feet away, told me a lot. And while he was relatively coherent, I wasn't sure how much of his surroundings were registering in his brain.

While I didn't give a smile, I did softly kiss his cheek. "Of course I'll stay with you." It was the least I could do. Logan's vulnerability was haunting me. I was so not used to seeing him in this condition.

As Logan held me, we watched the future Mrs. David Singleton compete in what seemed to be a never-ending dart match.

I was laughing at Loretta's most recent throw, two whole feet away from the board, when Logan suddenly said, "Hey, Christabel?"

"Yeah?" I asked, still watching the others. I wasn't anticipating intelligent conversation from him. Maybe he would ask for food. Maybe he'd ask me to get up so he could go use the rest room. Nothing major.

He moved his head closer to mine and whispered, "I love your beautiful hair." He gently removed my low ponytail then ran a hand through my curls.

"Oh! Thank you," I whispered back, leaning into him a little.

"I love your beautiful eyes and your beautiful face," he continued, stroking my hair and then my arm.

He often did that when we he was in a more loving mood. It was like a child's blanket to me. It instantly started me on the path to happiness. His touch was clumsy but still nice to feel. It was also another thing he hadn't given me in a while, a something I hadn't realized how much I missed. I shut my eyes for a moment, reveling in this feeling.

Logan moved so close to me, his lips grazed my ear. "And I love you."

My eyes rushed open, and I froze. Nothing existed anymore except Logan and his three little words. Not the loud people, not the blaring music. I couldn't even feel my body. Everything had been numbed into nonexistence.

I'd never expected to hear that from him. I wasn't sure I wanted to hear it.

We'd never come close to saying those words before. I was certain that if he meant it, he wouldn't have done it this way. He would have considered his current state and thought it very bad timing. He would have waited out the urge until the moment would no longer have the chance to be spoiled by what took place at the party.

I thought about how romantic the moment was supposed to be. Not in a corny way. Well, okay. Maybe the ideal fairytale "I love you" setting would involve twinkle lights and dozens of crimson-colored roses. Softly glowing candles everywhere. A string quartet hidden out of sight, playing beautiful a symphony. Logan in a suit and me in a frilly dress.

Life was not made up of perfect ideals, though. Life was typically made up of the next best things.

I could imagine that, too. There just needed to be a certain amount of sweetness. An understanding that, yes, the moment was real. The words were real. Even if it happened in the most unromantic setting. But I didn't think this most unromantic setting should include the other people, the bad music, and the alcohol.

And, oh my gosh, the alcohol. I figured he'd had about a gallon's worth, judging by his balance and slurring. If the amount was more than that, it wouldn't have surprised me in the least. I would have only been shocked if it was less.

Obviously, Logan wasn't big on romance. However, how could he have thought telling me this way was a good idea? I didn't even get the next best thing to my fantasy. To be honest, I felt cheated.

I thought about the repercussions of him meaning those three words. If that was how he'd tell me he loved me, how would he propose to me? In some dive bar with bad karaoke in the background? How was I going to explain this story to everyone? *"Well, he was completely trashed, and the words just popped out of his mouth."* Yeah, because that would leave me with a warm feeling inside.

It almost made me angry. Almost. The scene was too pitiful for me to truly be angry with Logan.

It had to be a lie. Well, it at least had to be something he never intended to say. Something that had never crossed his mind until the words were already out of his mouth. For all I knew, he didn't realize what he said.

I couldn't help but wonder what other fibs he might start telling when drunk. I finally believed this would not be the last time I would see him so intoxicated. Would he ever say an honest thing in this state?

I realized I had to say something back to him. First, though, I needed to force my organs to start functioning once more. My heart eventually began banging again. As the blood rushed through my veins and my surroundings became clear, every part of me asked, *What do I do?*

I slowly turned my head toward Logan, my nose less than an inch away from his. My breath was shallow, but I did have enough air to speak. I placed one hand on his shoulder closest to my body. The other softly rubbed his arm in a way similar to how he had been stroking mine.

"Logan, please don't say that," I whispered. "Not right now. Not like this. You're so drunk. It's not fair to say that to me now. We both know you don't mean it."

The cheerful, content expression on Logan's face dropped, but only for a minute. He stayed quiet, though.

I'd started to think maybe I should have said something different when he smiled, briefly kissed me on the lips, and gently removed me from his lap. He returned me to the chair before running upstairs. Afraid of what he was doing, I was stepping to follow him when he came back with two of the biggest cans of beer I'd ever seen plus one half-empty bottle of rum. My guess was that he'd chugged some of the rum on the way down, but I didn't know for sure.

He returned to our now empty chair and pulled a nearby footstool to him, on which he placed his handful of beverages. I walked over to him, but he ignored me. He popped the top on one of the cans, and off he went.

After ten minutes of Logan chugging as much as he could and another ten of me trying to get him to stop drinking, I was near my breaking point. Any sense my boyfriend possessed was nowhere in sight.

"I'm *fine*," he shrugged me off more than once. "Quit worrying. No big deal. Stop nagging me." That was followed by more laughs and swigs of liquor.

Is this my new boyfriend? I couldn't help but wonder. *He tells me he loves me yet won't accept my concern for him? Why the hell did I pick him over Eric?*

I asked David to keep Logan company while I ran upstairs for our jackets, taking what remaining alcohol Logan had with me. He was too drunk to chase after me, so he yelled at me as I walked away. After replacing the rum on the bar, I dumped what little was left of his beer. When I returned to the basement, I did a quick scan for the hostess.

"Hey, Loretta?" I began, pulling her aside. "It's been a great party, and I'm so happy we got to celebrate with you guys, but I think I'll take Logan home now."

She looked a little disappointed but definitely not surprised. "Yeah, that's probably best. How much has he had tonight?"

I rolled my eyes. "I doubt if he even knows. Is it okay if we leave his car here? We can pick it up first thing tomorrow morning."

"Absolutely! I don't want him driving like that." She moved her eyes toward our chair in the corner, where I knew Logan sat slumped and sulking. He was pissed with me for ruining his fun. His words, not mine.

"Thanks. You're not the only one." I looked Logan's way as well, knowing he couldn't possibly drive home in his condition and afraid if we didn't leave soon, he would try. David stood next to him, but Logan didn't seem like he wanted to talk to anyone.

David and I helped Logan drag himself up the stairs and outside to my car. It was a wobbly walk, but we got him seated in the front passenger side. I thanked David again before taking my place in the driver's seat. Logan had already fastened his seatbelt, so I did the same.

I turned the ignition, put the car in gear, and drove away as Logan sat beside me in distant silence.

Chapter Sixteen

Once we arrived at Logan's building, he and I quietly walked through the empty lobby to the elevators. After a brief and also quiet ride up to his floor, we stepped to Logan's door and stopped in front of it.

It was too late for any of his neighbors to be out except for the few that would certainly be gone until early the next morning. The stillness in the hallway was more than a little unsettling. I couldn't even hear any televisions blaring from inside the nearby apartments. It was just Logan and me standing in silence.

"Are you going to bed right now?" I finally asked, moving my eyes to him.

He shrugged. Barely. There was so little movement, I didn't think it could be considered an answer.

"Logan, I know today was crappy, but I'm sure tomorrow will be better."

Again, no answer. There had to be some way I could improve his mood.

I moved nearer to him, trying to get through the cold exterior he'd put up in order to find my true boyfriend. That man would still hold me. He would stay close to me, or as close as I would let him, even in the midst of an argument. When I wrapped my arms up around his neck, I couldn't tell if he was going to relax into me or not, but I had to hope.

"Maybe I should stay here tonight. I'm worried about you." I softly rubbed the back of his neck with my thumb, leaning myself into him a little.

Although Logan reciprocated the first gesture, putting his arms around my waist, he didn't look at me. "I don't need you to take care of me."

"I know, but I want to. Logan, what if you get sick or something? I don't want anything bad to happen to you."

"I'm fine," he sighed. There was a tinge of annoyance in his tone. While he hadn't relaxed like I'd hoped, he finally glanced at me.

I looked deeper into his eyes. The fog was gone by now, replaced by something that I couldn't quite decipher, something still different from what he expressed in the car. It was yet another thing I struggled to understand about him. How smug I was to think I knew anything about him at all. He was probably the single biggest mystery in my life.

"Are you sure?"

He nodded quietly.

I didn't know what else to say to him. I didn't know what I could say to make him feel better or to help him in some way. Everything I had tried failed. "Okay. Well, good night." I handed him his keys then leaned up and kissed his cheek.

When I moved back, he looked like he wanted to speak but reconsidered.

"Logan, is there something you—"

"Good night," he told me in a voice that was barely audible. After removing his remaining hand from me, he stepped back. He unlocked his apartment and walked in, waiting for me to leave so he could close the door.

"Okay, good night. I'll see you in the morning." I faked a smile. He didn't even try to kiss me before I left, which was out of character for him. Kissing at the door was one thing we always did no matter what.

After Logan shut the door, I sulked down the hall to the elevator. The whole ride to the lobby, I kept wondering where everything had gone off-track. How had my life turned into such a soap opera? When did every aspect of my life become so complicated?

I drove home in a state of confusion. My mind was poring over everything that had happened with Logan and Eric. I felt as if I'd heard the right things from the wrong people. That was ridiculous, though. I'd known Eric for about two seconds and Logan for more than half my life. I didn't want Eric telling me he was in love with me any more than I wanted Logan to.

I was pretty sure.

The next morning, after lounging around for an hour and drinking two cups of coffee, I called Logan at nine. Even with a massive hangover, I figured he'd be able to function at that hour.

"What's up?" he asked. His voice had no sleepiness to it at all—a good sign.

"Nothing much. How are you feeling today?" *Keep this light*, I told myself. *Perky and light. Don't say anything to piss him off.*

"I'm okay."

"That's good. So, no horrible hangover?"

"Nope."

I decided to get to my point. "I was wondering what time you want me to pick you up."

"What for?" he said through a mouthful of food.

"To get your car, silly. We left it at David and Loretta's. I told you last night I would pick you up to go get it. Or don't you remember?"

"Oh, that." He sounded as if I'd just reminded him to pick up his dry cleaning. No worry. No surprise. No remorse. No sign he remembered what occurred the night before. "I already got it."

I couldn't believe it. I hadn't been certain he was out of bed. The fact that he might have already left his house, picked up his car, and returned home definitely surprised me. I had to know for certain. "Oh! Um, okay. How did you get it? Did David and Loretta bring it to you or something?"

"Actually, Jesse picked me up a little while ago and took me. I didn't want to leave it at David's any longer than I had to."

"Oh, I see. Well, that's good that you have your car again." I felt stupid telling him that, but I honestly didn't know what else to say. Why had he been in such a rush to get his car? I knew for a fact he didn't need it until that evening at the earliest. And why hadn't he just called and told me? Had it not occurred to him that I might need this information? What if I hadn't called first and drove over to his place?

"Yeah. Look, I'm a little busy. I can't talk now. Call you later."

I heard the dial tone before I even had a chance to say bye. I didn't think he intentionally hung up on me but wasn't too sure.

As I ate my own breakfast of vanilla and honey-flavored Greek yogurt, I thought more about what happened the night before. Deciding to skip over Eric for the moment, I concentrated on my altered boyfriend. Until the party, I honestly never saw Logan like that. I knew he enjoyed an occasional beer or two, especially at get-togethers. But his drinking was usually drawn out over four or five hours, not four or five seconds.

However, nothing could have surprised me more than what he said to me in the basement. It had to be the liquor talking. It just *had* to. I couldn't find any other explanation for it. We had always been on the same path. Why change that?

By the time I emptied my yogurt cup, I was no closer to Logan enlightenment. I rinsed out the cup, dropped it in the recycling bin, washed my spoon, and still nothing. It seemed hopeless.

Since it was Saturday, I didn't have to go to work, and there were no meetings scheduled. I didn't have any work I could do at home. I was so excited about heading to the engagement party that I left the office without taking any files with me. I could have driven to the office to grab some things, but that didn't appeal to me.

I read issues of both newspapers I subscribed to. I also read a third online on my tablet then checked my work and personal email.

Still mentally blocked. Still bored.

I couldn't call Jetta because she wasn't supposed to be home all weekend. Alissa most likely had plans with Joe and probably wouldn't answer her phone.

I made a call to my sister in Michigan. Esmeralda, or Millie for short, was seven years older than me and often too busy to visit.

"How are things?" she asked.

Since I couldn't very well lie and say everything was great, I told her, "I'm not calling to talk about me. I want to know how you've been. I won't get to see you all until Christmas."

"Well, the kids have their winter holiday programs and concerts next week before break, and Chase is still looking for a new job. The quinceañera is going to be smaller and less expensive than Ana was hoping for. Much different than the parties you and I had. I was telling Mom the other day that..." Millie carried on talking, her stories distracting me from my currently miserable life.

Once my sis and I hung up, I watched a couple episodes of *Sex and the City,* including my favorite episode, when Carrie's Manolos are stolen. I'd forgotten how much I loved those shoes. The show didn't hold my interest for long, however. I started pacing around, growing more listless by the minute. No matter how many times I checked my phone, there were no missed calls. Logan's phone kept going to voice mail.

I wasn't hungry for lunch; it was too early to start dinner. I didn't have much food for dinner, anyway. I had been working too much to shop. That sounded like a great plan, though. I threw on boots, gloves, a scarf, and a coat and headed outside. I walked the few blocks to my local grocery store, deeply breathing in the crisp air. Luckily, the sidewalks were precipitation-free, no snow around to crunch through. Not too long after, I walked home again with all the ingredients I needed to make homemade blueberry muffins and something delicious for an actual dinner, not a frozen microwavable one.

I couldn't remember the last time I had a long enough spare moment to make homemade food. And, for the moment, I chose to forget the fact that the only reason I knew how to cook so well was because of Logan's lessons.

Soon, the deliciously sweet aroma of warming muffin batter began to fill the kitchen, eventually wafting out to the other rooms of my little apartment. Though I still wasn't hungry, I waited impatiently for the muffins to bake. I didn't know how else to pass the time. I couldn't seem to let myself enjoy the break. I needed something to keep me occupied and was exhausting my options.

Many hours later, I eventually went to bed happy in the knowledge that the day was almost over. Despite everything I'd accomplished, there was one thing I had no control over: Logan never called.

Chapter Seventeen

Sunday came and went in the slowest passage of time *ever*. Logan called me late Sunday morning, only to tell me he had family plans all day and couldn't talk. We spoke for no more than five minutes, if that. I understood that he was busy, but I wanted more. There was an important discussion we needed to have.

Of course, I didn't mention that to Logan. It didn't feel like the right time.

There was something I couldn't quite name invading my mind, infecting my every thought and feeling. It nagged at me without identifying itself, leaving me to ignore it as best as I could.

By Tuesday afternoon, I was not only excruciatingly bored but also moody and still confused. I'd spent the past two days rarely leaving the realm of tedium. My boyfriend wasn't in a hurry to see me or talk to me. I had no idea what in the world was going on with him.

The weather had settled into a nice steadiness of melting, gray-colored blah. I detested my work environment.

I hated my mood. I hated the weather. I hated having to be at work. I was *thisclose* to hating Logan. Everything and everyone sucked.

Frankly, I was a miserable mess.

After absently "working" through lunch, I found myself in one of my quiet funks again. Jetta found me there, too. She'd watched me from her desk for about ten minutes before walking over to mine with an apprehensiveness I wasn't used to seeing from her. It was more than the lip biting or hair twirling. She took her time getting over to me, a first for her.

"Hey, Chrissie!" She smiled, but it didn't do much to hide the worry in her face.

"Hey, Jetta!" I smiled weakly in return, glancing up from the work I was still pretending to do.

What I had actually been busy with was figuring out the artist of the last song I heard before I left my car that morning. My radio had been on the fritz so I couldn't read the words on the display. The song was stuck in my head, and it was driving me crazy that I couldn't remember. I didn't remember the title, either, or I would have looked it up online.

I almost teased Jetta about wrinkles forming with that much of a scrunched expression, but I held back. I wanted to lighten her mood, not make her worry more. "What's going on?"

"Well, I was about to ask you the same thing."

I had yet to talk to Logan about the engagement party. He would have been mortified if I told someone else, especially Jetta.

"I'm okay. I'm not feeling all that well right now." While that wasn't the complete truth, it was enough to keep me from feeling too guilty about not being upfront about the whole Logan situation.

"Is it like a stomach thing?" she asked with a sympathetic face. "I heard a lot of the other departments are catching some sort of virus. It's slowly circulating its way through the entire building. There are at least two or three people on every floor who have caught it, including Alissa's team. She just came back Thursday. Almost everyone that had it missed at least a week of work because of it."

Crap. I thought there was a reason Alissa didn't look so great the last time I saw her. No wonder she asked me to send her some files. She was probably worried she'd fallen behind. And how did I not notice Alissa's absence? Jetta really was going to worry about me.

"I'm sure it's not that," I smiled the best I could. Of course, my stomach starting hurting for real. "I'll be all right. I'm feeling a little slower than normal. A little more tired, too. I haven't been sleeping much. Nothing a good nap couldn't take care of."

"Are you sure?"

"Yep. I think a nap would definitely cure me." Actually, a nap sounded good at the moment. If I knew how to take one at work without getting caught, I totally would have tried.

"Okay. If you say so. But if you need me for anything, I'm only twenty feet away." She glanced at her watch. "Well, in about an hour, Alissa and I are going to strategize at the coffee house down the street. Come over in about forty-five minutes if you want to join us."

She went back to her desk as I honestly tried to focus on my work. What else was I going to do if I couldn't sleep?

Since the client had loved that morning's pitch, our project moved on to the art department for a few extra additions before publication. Robert and I immediately joined the rest of our creative team on the new assignment. Unfortunately, I had no opportunity to be relieved by this. Mari had made it perfectly clear to me that my job was on the line if I stayed disposable in her eyes.

I already had a stack of copy I'd turned in late Friday sitting on my desk, waiting for revisions. If I'd thought about it, I could have kept myself busy over the weekend working on the new campaign. But I hadn't had my laptop, forgetting it at work in the rush of trying to get to the party on time.

I flipped through the pages, unhappy to see red marks on every page. Some things were crossed out, others circled with question marks nearby. On some, nothing was written other than *Not usable* or *Not what client wants.*

As creatives, we were encouraged to embrace failure. We were supposed to view it as an important tool. "Failure is simply a way of weeding out the bad ideas in order to find the great ones," our old CD explained to us daily.

I learned a long time before I ever started at Madison not to take negative remarks personally, but it was difficult to remember such sage advice at the moment. It was difficult to embrace my blatant failure. Even though I hadn't worked long on those ideas, I still thought they were good. Apparently, Mari didn't agree.

It could be such a pain in the butt trying to please other people. When I was a little girl, my dad always told me that it was impossible to please everyone. That some people will just not like you or what you are offering them. That some folks will never be happy. He said the only thing to do is your best.

Of course, that was easy for him to say. For as long as I could remember, he ran operations for a local furniture company. He never dealt directly with customers or even with bosses above him. My father's advice was no help to me now.

In my eyes, I did exactly what was asked of me. How was I supposed to improve on that? Sure, my concepts could use tweaking on a few details, but I didn't see anything wrong with the overall designs. From what I understood, they were great concepts that our client would love.

I wasn't sure of what to do or how to proceed. I glanced across the room to Jetta for help, but she was furiously typing on her keyboard, not having left yet. Seeing her so focused at least gave me the confidence that our campaign would be fine without anyone else's help—in other words, mine. It was a great thing to behold when Jetta concentrated on work and work alone.

Unwilling to interrupt her, I looked back at my own work, my brain completely out of thoughts. When I created those ideas, I had been focusing on not one but two projects that day. Of course my concepts about a new client made on the day of my presentation weren't going to be outstanding.

I stared at the sheet of paper directly in front of me. The longer I stared, the more my eyes began to sort of glaze over. I eventually couldn't distinguish anything except the haze of black blobs on white paper.

I must have stared blankly at my computer screen for half an hour when I heard my CD's voice in front of me.

"Christabel! How are things coming along?" Mari asked with a broad smile.

She wore a pantsuit and fabulous high heels—I knew this without looking. Though she was in her early forties, she looked young enough to fit in with the twenty-somethings of the agency.

She moved her eyes to my stack of papers, then back to me.

Double crap. From the expression on Mari's face, I knew I was busted for slacking on the job. She didn't understand the concept of giving your mind a refreshing break. I knew she was wondering why I wasn't typing as furiously as Jetta.

"Uh, things are coming along nicely." I grinned.

Okay, so I lied. But I couldn't exactly tell her, "You know, I haven't done any work today. At all. And I don't have plans to do any for quite some time." Talking to Mari like that was a quick path to unemployment. Not a place I was ready to go yet.

"I take it you've been working on your revisions." Mari's eyes narrowed almost imperceptibly, yet her face remained calm.

"Of course," I fibbed some more, holding my smile as I picked up the top piece of paper to somehow reinforce my answer.

"Good." Mari held her smile as well. It was a taut, intimidating, powerful sort of grin that said, "You better not be lying to me or else." It didn't help that her eyes revealed the same train of thought as her mouth.

Needless to say, her expression frightened me to my core. After the way she'd humiliated me, I hated her, yes. But I still feared her. Mari held power that could ruin my future.

"You must have been busy on those revisions all morning, huh? I was happy to see you worked all through your lunch hour."

I silently nodded. I had accidentally stayed at my desk for the whole day, but work had nothing to do with it. I was afraid of what she would say next. There was also a big possibility that if I had to lie any more, I was going to crack.

"I'm hopeful to have something new to look at by the end of the day. I'm leaving a little early and won't be able to wait all night for submissions." Translation: "You better bust your ass to finish those right *now*."

"I'm also interested to see how your thought process plays those out." She glanced at the revision stack again.

Oh shit, she's going to slit my throat with her stiletto Louboutins, isn't she? "Of course. The gears are already turning. Have been all day."

Hmm. Guess I had more lies in me.

"Paolo has been meeting with some clients all day long, but I guaranteed him that he would have new material to look at first thing tomorrow. This client," Mari tapped her blood red dragon talon on the paper stack, "is anxious to move beyond the early stages of what they've seen. I expect you want your work to be part of that."

"Oh, absolutely! Things aren't quite ready yet, but they will be very soon. I promise."

"Good," she replied before walking away.

I was nowhere near finishing any revisions, let alone submitting them to her. Why did I have to lie to her? Why had I been so terrified to be truthful? I completely screwed myself. Now I had to do real, honest-to-goodness work. A *lot* of it.

Even though I had no idea where to start, I forced myself to focus on at least some aspect of the revisions. I picked up a few more sheets of paper and immediately got started. I wrote. I read. I wrote some more. I made a million scribbles and barely legible notes on the papers and typed it all into the computer. I never went to the coffee shop with Jetta and Alissa. I didn't know when they left, and I didn't know when or if they returned.

All I could think about was saving my job, even if it was a job I hated. I could not bear losing it when I had the power to keep it. Two hours after Mari's stare-down, I'd reworked a handful of usable revisions for both Mari and Paolo to read.

By the time I left the building to find my car, my previous bad feeling had turned into something so dreadful, it made me nauseated. I'd submitted work that was so far from being the greatest that good wasn't even on its radar. Until that point, I'd never turned in anything that I didn't believe was the best I could do.

I had already begun resenting the fact that all the people around me seemed to be creative geniuses. I just knew they were going to end up with all the ad campaigns while I was going to end up with nothing but an empty portfolio and a grudge.

On top of it all, I was kissing goodbye any shot at promotion.

Chapter Eighteen

After a similar day at work on Wednesday and still no word from my boyfriend since Sunday, I decided I wouldn't wait for things to happen anymore. Waiting hadn't given me anything but an uncertain mind and a weak stomach. I was done with waiting.

While blankly staring at my computer screen yet again, I'd had a brilliant idea, only it wasn't about work. It was about Logan. There was something I knew I could do that might get him to open up to me or at least get him to speak to me. I wasn't sure if his avoidance was intentional, but I had to try something.

Instead of heading home after work, I stopped and ordered a large pepperoni pizza from Logan's favorite pizzeria. It was the place he'd taken me on our first official date. The pizzeria was a good twenty minutes beyond his typical restaurant circuit, but it was well worth the journey. While the pizza cooked, I debated walking to a nearby grocery store to grab a bottle of red wine but decided against it. Even though we'd shared a bottle that first night, it didn't seem like a good idea to head that direction. Alcohol had played such a huge part in recent events.

I also picked up a disc of the film we watched in the local movie theater that night, choosing to buy the movie so we could see it whenever we wanted. I could have easily streamed it but wanted physical proof to show him that I tried.

Without knowing if Logan was home, I drove to his apartment. If he was home, I wanted to force him to see me and not give him the chance to ignore me.

Not that he would really ignore me, right?

After parking my car, I freshened up my lip gloss and pulled out a blotting paper to dab at my T-zone. I grabbed what I needed and walked inside. As quickly as I could, I rushed to the elevator to head upstairs, the warmth of the pizza spreading into my hand along the way. The elevator felt like it took absolutely forever to go up three measly floors. I could have run up the stairs faster than that. I probably should have. Nothing could get me to Logan's fast enough. When the elevator doors finally opened, I practically sprinted to his apartment.

At his door, I knocked twice and waited patiently. As I stood in front of his apartment, my heart began to race. It beat so fast I thought it might explode. Then my hands started to tremble. I had to tighten my grip on the pizza box to steady them.

I couldn't believe how much I missed him. It was a feeling I'd never experienced before. Even during our week of silence last June, I was mad at him so much more than I actually missed him.

And obviously, this was all completely selfless. It had nothing to do with the fact that Eric didn't want to see me anymore. Or because I was still reeling from that. Of course not. This was about Logan. He needed me, whether or not he knew that. He needed me to prove to him that he hadn't ruined things. That I still cared. I couldn't let him down.

The only problem was that I wasn't sure how willing he would be to see things from my perspective. It was about more than his stubbornness. He was in a vulnerable place. I'd bruised his ego. Unfortunately, I had no idea how to break through that wall he used to hide from me.

My nervousness started making me feel sick. There were so many uncertainties and possible outcomes of the night that my brain didn't know what to focus on. This was so not a time I could enjoy the element of surprise.

About thirty seconds later, Logan finally answered the door. He wore only a sweater and jeans, no socks, which told me he hadn't planned on leaving the apartment that night. And since I didn't smell any cooking aromas wafting out from the kitchen, I definitely knew I'd made the perfect plans for us.

"Hi!" I smiled, quickly leaning in to kiss his slightly scruffy cheek. "I'm so glad you're home."

His shock at seeing me was clear. I wasn't going to let that affect me. Besides, it was too early to tell if he was happy about this surprise appearance. He'd opened the door a little wider but hadn't invited me in.

"What are you doing here, Christabel?"

"I wanted to surprise you." I showed him what I held in my hands. "I thought we could re-create our first date. Doesn't that sound like fun?"

"Oh, yeah. Real fun."

His sarcasm instantly deflated my bubble of hope. My smile dropped from its perch and stopped halfway down. Okay, so the shock wasn't a happy one.

The bitterness in his tone really stung me. I hadn't prepared myself for such indifference. However, I wasn't entirely ready to give up. What kind of message would it give him if I did?

I gave Logan the best smile I could muster. "You've wanted to see this movie again for ages. And this is your favorite pizza. With extra sauce and extra cheese and lots of breadsticks on the side." I opened the box to show him, a sort of grand demonstration of my thoughtfulness. As I did so, the yummy pizza smells began filling the air around us.

Logan glanced at the pizza then back at me. He was not giving me the best smile he could muster. In fact, he wasn't smiling at all. "Look, I don't feel like doing this right now."

I slammed the box shut. "Like doing what exactly? I'm asking you to share dinner and a movie with your girlfriend. That's, what? A whole two hours of your night? At most? It shouldn't require much effort. You should be happy to spend that time with me."

"So, what? *Now* you want to be the perfect girlfriend? You're kidding me, right?"

There was so much derision in his tone that my heart started to pound. It wasn't from excitement or even the hope of it but the feeling of impending doom.

I often held my tongue in the past, well before the World Series party, rarely ever vocalizing my unhappiness with him and to him. I hated fighting. It didn't usually seem worth it to me. But I couldn't do that again. Holding back had never led me to anything I wanted or needed. It never cured my confusion.

The frustration I felt this time had me ready to storm off and forget about him. I knew I deserved better than this. I didn't want to acknowledge someone who would act in such a way. My hurting ego, however, told me to fight back if this was how he was going to treat me.

"Why are you doing this to me? You've never been so insensitive before, which is saying a lot. This is *you* we're talking about. Things were becoming pretty great between us. Why would you mess with that? What has gotten into you?"

He gave a sort of laugh, but it was riddled with sarcasm. "*I'm* the insensitive one?"

"Yes. You are."

My eyes felt hot, but I refused to yield to that. I didn't want to cry. I wanted to lash out. I wanted him to hurt, too. I wanted him to feel how painful it was to be trampled on and kicked over like he'd done to me. This was no time to be sad; it was a time to get even.

Though I'd already stopped talking, I couldn't help adding, "Maybe you can teach me how to make such a quick transformation. It seems to be pretty easy to become such a jerk. All in a snap, right? Nice guy." I snapped my fingers. "Asshole." I snapped again. "Nice guy." *Snap!* "Jerk face. I mean, that is how you do it, isn't it?"

The look he gave me almost made me recoil. "Yeah, that's exactly what I do, Christabel."

"It is! It is exactly what you do. I never know when you're going to adore me and when you're going to ignore me. You are the most unpredictable person I know. And so not in a good way. Never in a good way."

He silently glared at me.

"What happened to you?" I continued in my rant. "You used to be so kind to me when we were friends. Why is that guy just gone now?"

"What happened to me?" Logan asked with an unflinching stare. "What the hell happened to you? You used to be my friend, too. When did you turn into such an unfeeling person?"

I opened my mouth to retaliate, then sighed. Lashing out sucked, too. How was anything going to make me feel better? There had to be some kind of perfect balance—a compromise of what we both needed and wanted.

After another sigh, I looked to Logan again. "This is not what I wanted to do tonight. You're being a jerk; I'm being a jerk. And for what? It's stupid. I didn't mean to be so cruel. I'm feeling a little frayed right now. I'm sure you would say the same. I think we should take a little time to cool off, and we can re-create our fabulous first date tomorrow. How does that sound?"

I offered up a small smile, fully expecting him to nod. "It sounds perfect," he would say, and smile as well. "Exactly what we need."

Only he didn't smile.

Still leaning with his hands against the doorframe, Logan shook his head and bore his eyes into me. "Stop pretending, okay? Just stop it!"

I shifted uncomfortably. "What are you talking about? I'm not pretending anything."

His voice grew louder as he spoke. "Are you kidding me? You're acting like everything has been okay between us. Like we've been some perfect, happy couple, and we haven't. Not even close. You cannot just make shit up in your head and go, 'Yeah, that's how it is.'"

"I don't."

"Christabel, do you even remember what happened Friday night?"

"Yes. Of course, I do," I answered, thinking, *Do you remember what happened that night?* "But I don't understand what that has to do with now."

"How can you not understand? I told you that I *love* you."

All the breath I had got knocked out of me. Everything in sight started swirling into a blur. *Wait a minute... What?? He didn't... I mean, did he...*

"You said nothing in return."

So, he actually knew *he... Oh my...!* I had no idea what to do with this information. Nothing came to mind except the question of what in the world had just happened.

I opened my mouth to say what exactly I wasn't sure when Logan added, "Oh, wait! I forgot. You did say something. You told me not to say that to you. That I wasn't being fair to you. You even accused me of not meaning it."

My strength and my breath returned enough for me to reply. "Well, technically, I said the situation you put me in wasn't fair."

"Is that really any different?"

"Yes, actually, it—"

"Either way, you made it perfectly clear you didn't want to hear it."

With a heavy sigh, I replied, "Logan, what was I supposed to think? You'd ingested more alcohol than the entire 'Jersey Shore' cast did in one week. No one would have believed you in that moment."

We silently stared at each other for a few seconds as Logan shifted uncomfortably. I started mentally preparing everything I wanted to say to him. Every question, every comment. He wasn't the only one who needed answers about the past. First and foremost in my mind was what happened that Friday. He had to account for his behavior. We would never figure out anything without understanding that night.

I did the only thing I could do. I waited for Logan to break the silence.

When he spoke again, his voice had a surprising softness to it. "I didn't say it because of the alcohol. I tried telling you long before Friday, but I got... well, honestly, I got scared."

Whoa! Logan admitting he was scared was a major deal. He had never admitted that to me before. I couldn't imagine the kind of strength it took for him to say it. I nearly fell to the floor from shock. I didn't have a free hand to pinch myself, but I sunk my teeth into my bottom lip hard enough to know it wasn't a dream.

My voice grew softer, too. "You did? When?"

"One night in your hallway."

I had to think for a moment. We'd been in my hallway about a thousand times during our relationship. How was I supposed to know which time he meant? And then it hit me: the first night of David's World Series parties. That moment the ever-confident Logan didn't seem very sure of what he wanted to say.

"Oh my goodness," I whispered. I felt the need to sit, but dropping down to the hallway floor did not appeal to me.

"Yeah," he nodded. "I've felt it for a long time now but didn't know how to tell you. You were always going on about how committed we were without being serious. But I was serious. I *am* serious about you."

All that time together, all those dates, and I'd had no idea. I felt so stupid for having been clueless. "You never said anything. Why?"

He shrugged. "I guess I kept hoping that at some point, you'd feel for me the way I feel for you. I realize it was dumb to tell you the way I did on Friday. I feel awful about that. I feel awful about all of it. I was such an idiot that night."

I wanted to nod but didn't. He'd granted me my wish. He was finally opening up to me. I would be the idiot if I threw that away.

I took a deep breath and subconsciously held it as he continued, "So, I'm going to try again. Soberly. I owe it to you. To us."

"Oh my goodness," I repeated quietly. Once out loud and about a million times in my head.

There were no twinkle lights or rose bouquets, but there was definitely the feeling that this was real. That, yes, this was *the* moment.

However, I wasn't sure I was prepared for it.

Although Logan didn't touch me, he did bridge the gap between us. He was so close that all I could smell was his cologne. I watched his eyes and face and began to tremble.

Here it comes, I thought. *Am I ready?*

"I love you, Christabel."

I looked up into his eyes again and saw what every woman dreamed of seeing. Warmth. Passion. *Love*. Why hadn't I noticed it before?

I didn't know what to do. I clutched the movie case in my left hand, searching my mind and my heart for an answer.

I thought about what life would be like if I told Logan I loved him. I was sure he would take me in his arms and kiss me unendingly. He'd be overjoyed. He would probably be thrilled to settle for the pizza and movie as long as he could be with the one he loved.

But how would I feel?

I thought I knew exactly what would happen if I didn't return Logan's declaration of love. I would become number one on his most hated list. He would tell Jesse, who would call me awful names and say Logan was better off without me. They would badmouth me in every conversation for weeks. Logan's hatred of me would only grow.

Confusion and animosity would filter out through the rest of our friends. Some of them would take sides, though I couldn't figure out where most of the blame would land. It was safe to assume there would be no more group hangouts, no more parties, and no more fun. My life would become a total nightmare.

Was that what I wanted? Was it even something I could handle?

The truth was hiding somewhere in between the layers and layers of uncertainty. What did I really, truly want? More to the point, what did I feel?

I mean, love is powerful. "I love you" is a powerful phrase. It's one of the first things our parents say to us after we're born. It's one of the very first things we hear. It is also often one of the last things people say to relatives and significant others before dying. We say "I love you" to family, to close friends, to those who mean the most to us. That phrase is not to be taken lightly, not to be used without the meaning behind it, and not to be spoken if not true. As far as I was concerned, anyway.

Finally, I asked Logan in a gentle tone, "You really love me?"

"Yeah. I really do."

I parted my lips to speak, but nothing came out. No words, not even any unintelligible mumbling or nervous squeaks. I quickly shut my lips again.

Running through my mind were the replies my loved ones would tell me to say. The advice those dear to me would give. My mom, my dad, my sister, Jetta.

"You cannot say it if you don't mean it." My mother's wise words.

Of course, my father would say that I was too young to commit myself to any man. That I needed to focus on me and me only. *"Love will only get in your way."* This had pretty much been my way of thinking up to this point.

My sister would give me advice but nothing to sway me one way or the other. *"It's easy. Three words: I. love. You. No biggie. If you feel it, say it. Do what feels right to you."*

And Jetta, well... Jetta would be Jetta. *"Love him? Fantastic! Don't love him? So what? You can easily find someone new."*

Then there was Eric's voice, not with an answer but a question. A question that echoed from my brain to my heart. *"Do you love Logan?"*

I needed my own voice, my own answer. No more questions.

Logan waited expectantly. "And?"

"And I... really care about you."

Dead silence. Unwavering stare. Lots of nervous curse words in my head.

"That's it?" he asked calmly and slowly, tilting his head a little. "You *care* about me?"

Oh crap. Oh crap! I smiled. "Well, of course I care about you. I missed you, too. I've wanted to see you for days. I wanted to call you, too, but I wasn't sure how busy you were. I wasn't sure about that before I came over, either. Obviously. I knew it was a risk, but I didn't want to wait anymore. I had to see you because I haven't in days, and I missed you."

Halfway through, I realized I was rambling. And I knew why.

"Is there anything else you want to say?" he asked when I was done. His eyes had glazed over, and his jaw looked clenched. Not enough that others would have noticed, but I saw it.

That angry face had me completely freaked out. I said so many swear words in my mind that I would have to wear those hideous bracelets for the next four weeks. I just kept wondering, *How can I make things better?*

"Logan, please don't—" I began before he shook his head, holding up a hand to stop me.

A note of sarcasm returned. "I'm sorry. The response we were looking for is 'I love you, too.'"

I involuntarily winced. "But Logan, I—"

"No. I can't do this anymore. And I think you need to leave. Now."

He gently took me by the shoulders, holding on for a second before moving me back about a foot or so. He stood in the doorway, waiting for me to walk away. Again. Only this time, we didn't have plans for the morning. We didn't have plans for any time in the future. Ever.

I'd barely stepped another foot down the hall when I heard the door slam behind me.

Chapter Nineteen

Somehow, I realized I was in my car, still holding on to the pizza and movie case. An unknown amount of time had passed between my entering the car and finally becoming aware of it. I was so dumbstruck that I had no idea what to think. Honestly, I wasn't doing much thinking.

I started the engine on instinct, pulling out of my parking spot without seeing anything around me. Nothing registered in my brain. My car, along with my limbs, did the thinking for me because I wasn't able to do it myself. My mind had shut down. I couldn't cope with anything more than driving home on autopilot.

At my building, I parked the car, walked upstairs, and entered my apartment. Every move I made was slow and deliberate. I remembered to hang up my purse on the coat rack, taking my time as I walked three feet to the living room. Gingerly, I set on the coffee table the pizza I would never eat and the movie I never wanted to see again. With a small sigh, I dropped onto the sofa, never bothering to remove my outerwear. I didn't really notice any of it.

Thousands of emotions began flowing through me for the first time since leaving Logan's. The shock was gone. And in its place came hurt, anger, confusion, frustration, remorse, sadness. And then there was the guilt.

Oh, the guilt! Guilt for liking Eric. Guilt for not loving Logan the way he wanted me to or even at all. Guilt for not noticing what I should have about my boyfriend.

It was horribly painful feeling all those emotions at once. It was like systematically being broken into a billion little pieces while at the same time being crushed by a thousand-ton boulder as wild animals ripped me to shreds. Every new thought hurt worse than the last.

In order to make it stop, I wanted what a lot of people did in times like this: a quick way to shut everything out, even if temporarily.

A desperate urge to consume alcohol started growing inside me, but heavy drinking had played a part in my misery.

Then I felt an intense need to shop. Shoe shopping, purse shopping, furniture shopping, it didn't matter. Even grocery shopping would have worked in that moment if I bought the special, nonessential things like the fancy imported foods I never bothered to treat myself with. Or some of those cute, little ceramic vases or collectible animal figurines they kept in the gift and flower section. Flowers would have worked, too. Bright, happy-colored ones with intense fragrances.

Unfortunately, I didn't have spare money to spend on recreational shopping sprees. I barely had enough money for basic grocery shopping.

The only thing left to do was cry. So, I did.

I cried for hours, maybe. I wasn't sure how long. While sitting on my sofa, I held my face in my hands and let it all out. I sobbed for everything I felt, everything Logan felt, even everything Eric felt. I cried enough tears to fill an Olympic-size swimming pool.

As I wept, there was a tiny, little part of me that thought Logan wasn't crying over me. That maybe, just maybe, he was congratulating himself for finally getting rid of me. That he was happy he wasn't stuck with me anymore. He was free to go find his perfect woman—the woman who would be so much better than me in a million different ways.

Of course, I immediately regretted this, knowing I thought this only to make myself feel better about what happened to us.

But, honestly, there was something to it. If I thought he could find a woman superior to me, everything we'd gone through wouldn't matter. There would be no more guilt for me to suffer through. No more sadness. The rain clouds of heartbreak would clear away. I could tell Logan, "So what if we broke up? You're in love with the perfect woman now. She loves you, too. Who cares what happened between the two of us?"

Despite my desire to make our reality different, though, it *did* matter. What we had and how we ended mattered. More than I ever imagined it would.

I couldn't stop picturing the pain in Logan's face. I knew it was an expression of the pain in his heart and quickly silenced that selfish, bitter part of me.

When I finally felt like I had no tears left to shed, I picked myself up off the couch and shuffled into the kitchen for a tall glass of water. There was nothing like crying your eyes out to make you thirsty and dehydrated. I slowly removed a glass from the cabinet, filling it with water I kept in the fridge. The shock of such cold liquid tightened my throat, but I kept swallowing. This pain was more bearable than the demise of my relationship.

As I downed my water, I ignored the picture of Logan and me on the fridge and another in a white frame next to the far window. I had no desire to remember how happy we once were, no wish to see our smiling faces staring back at me. It made me weak enough catching the smallest of glimpses of the photo on the refrigerator. Seeing the entire picture probably would have collapsed me to the floor.

I returned to the living room with my freshly refilled water glass, stopping short of the sofa to find the remnants of my ruined plans staring back from the coffee table.

The pizza had been out for what I guessed was about five hours by this time. Even if it hadn't sat out, I still didn't want it. I traded my glass for the pizza box and movie, taking them to the kitchen. I opened my garbage can lid and set the pizza inside, placing the DVD on top of the box. I replaced the lid and walked away. Then I stopped after a few steps.

Was it necessary to throw them both away?

Well, of course it was. The pizza was cold. I never wanted to see that movie again. It would only make me think of Logan. Yet I couldn't throw it in the trash, could I?

I debated for another minute or two before returning to the garbage can. I gingerly lifted the lid and removed the movie case. In very smooth motions, I wiped it down with a disinfecting wipe and washed my hands. I took the DVD case with me back to the living room. After adding it to my perfectly disorganized collection, I curled onto the sofa, jacket, shoes, and all.

Picking up the remote control, I clicked on the television, more for noise than anything. If you asked me, I couldn't tell you what aired. I didn't pay attention to it. I also didn't pay attention to how long it was before I fell asleep.

The next morning, I woke up in the same position, never having moved in the night. My head throbbed; my eyes burned. It took eons for my stiff legs to painfully stretch out from their curl. I was still so exhausted that I couldn't tell how much I'd slept. Honestly, I felt hung over.

I popped my swollen eyes open, noticing a bright fuzz making the most incredible noise in front of me. Then it became clear. The TV was still on, blaring out some "magic cooking" infomercial. Not something I wanted to deal with first thing in the morning.

It felt like the presenters and their "audience" were in the living room with me. Annoyed, I groggily hit the "Off" button.

After rubbing my bleary eyes, I heaved myself up to sitting. The sunlight shone through little cracks in my blinds, causing my eyes to take a few seconds to adjust. I'd barely turned any lights on when I got home the night before. The darkness had added a strange form of comfort. But now the room seemed as bright as if all the lights were on at the same time. Maybe more so. Or maybe it was my screwy vision.

I was in the middle of blinking my eyes awake when I caught sight of my clock. 6:38. *Crap!* I was so unbelievably late! It was well over an hour after I normally woke up. I didn't want to think about how much the traffic would add to my time.

Sprinting to my bathroom, I quickly stripped before showering at lightning speed. Once out, I applied very basic makeup before brushing my teeth and hair. I ran across the little hall to the bedroom, wrapped in a towel, tiny beads of water falling from me as I moved. Without thinking much about what to wear, I dressed and headed for the door, grabbing my bag and coat along the way. Though I was in a rush, I still managed to grab those stupid SWBs I was supposed to wear.

From the time I woke up to the time I left, only about eleven or so minutes had passed—a new record for me. Normally, I would have been thrilled about getting ready so quickly. But this was definitely not the kind of morning I wanted to remember. I no longer had a boyfriend, I was late for work, I wore a pantsuit because I couldn't remember the last time I shaved my legs, and I felt my mascara clumping in the corner of one eye.

As I zipped along the roads to the Eisenhower expressway, I realized I'd forgotten to eat breakfast. Not only did I not have breakfast, I hadn't eaten dinner the night before.

Thank goodness traffic flowed so smoothly. My drive in to the city was faster than it had been in a long time. Of course, this could have had something to do with my speed, but I chose to think I was well within the legal limits.

I found a parking spot easily and within walking distance to work, so at least a few things were going right.

Inside, I smiled and waved to Eleanor, hurrying to the elevators before she scolded me for arriving ten minutes after seven.

Once I left the elevator, I intended to head straight for my desk. I would sort through my returned submissions, check my work email, and pull up my favorite brainstorming program on the computer. For the next several hours, I would become the single best copywriter ever. Nothing would get in my way. As long as I made it to my own desk. Straight there; no distractions.

I headed straight for Jetta's.

"Hey!" She smiled, moving her eyes up to me from the computer screen. It was obvious she was having a good morning. Her face was full of perkiness. Then she really looked at me, and all her happiness faded away. "Chrissie, what happened to you? You're so pale. Are you okay?"

I hadn't planned on telling her. I wasn't sure what she would think. But the moment I opened my mouth, I blurted out, "He loved me."

Chapter Twenty

"Who did?" Jetta asked with growing concern. She rose from her chair and walked around to me.

"He loved me, and now he hates me," I replied, not paying attention to her. My mind began flashing back to the night before. The expressions on Logan's face, the scorn in his voice. It was all still so fresh, it caused my body to shake violently from the rising emotions.

"*Who*?" she asked again. "Eric?"

I darted my eyes to her face. "What? No! *Logan*." As I said his name, my legs wobbled underneath me. I leaned against Jetta's desk to steady myself.

Jetta watched me, my strange behavior finally making sense to her. After a second or two, she took my purse from my hand and placed it by her own bag. "Come with me," she said, turning me around toward the corridor.

Robert walked up to us as we turned. His dark brows furrowed, and we halted our footsteps.

While his physique wasn't intimidating—he was only about an inch or two taller than me, and I'm 5'5"—his demeanor could be. I swear the building itself trembled when he was angry. It was a frightening thing. Other than the clients, obviously, the first three people my co-workers tried to keep the happiest were Mari, Robert, and Paolo, in that order.

"Where are you going?" Robert's voice bellowed at us. We were close enough that he could have whispered, and we still would have heard him.

"We're going to the ladies' room," Jetta answered with a small smile. "Christabel isn't feeling all that well." She sent a sympathetic look my way, but Robert didn't seem to notice.

His tone remained harsh. "Now is not a good time."

"What does that mean?" I asked him.

"Mari's freaking out over this new client that isn't happy about anything. She has meetings and conference calls scheduled with clients and AEs in addition to all our team meetings."

Jetta glanced at me and almost imperceptibly rolled her eyes. "So? What exactly does that have to do with us?"

"Everyone is supposed to work all day. We have to stay at our desks. There is no time for slacking off."

"I wouldn't call feeling ill 'slacking off.' That would imply Christabel is intentionally avoiding her work, which she isn't. Or is this too sensible for you to understand?" Jetta gave him a saucy, defiant smile.

Robert's displeasure meant nothing to Jetta. I knew she viewed it as his problem, not ours. I also knew his condescending attitude infuriated her.

I could tell Robert was fuming by this point. His face was as red as I'd ever seen it. With clenched teeth, he replied, "Return to your desks."

Jetta never flinched. She certainly was not one to back down when on a mission. Her smile grew wider, her voice syrupy sweet. "We won't be doing that. So, Christabel can either throw up in the bathroom like a normal person or right here next to you and your brand new Italian leather shoes. It's your choice."

Jetta kindly rubbed my arm as Robert glanced back and forth between us. He didn't look like he was buying it. Jetta's face remained the same, but I saw panic in her eyes. We tried to keep Robert happy, but he had overstepped the boundary between acting like a boss and being bossy.

I decided to play along and swallowed hard, putting my hands on my stomach. I even hunched over a bit. "Where should I go?" I moaned pitifully, trying to sound as ill as I could.

Robert looked like he wanted to throw up. "Bathroom. *Please*." He grimaced and quickly walked away.

"That was fun!" Jetta laughed as she half-dragged me to the bathroom closest to our section.

It was pretty fun. I had never seen Robert so discomfited before. However, there were other things demanding attention.

Once we were safely inside the restroom, Jetta said, "Okay. What happened? Start from the beginning. Tell me everything."

So, I did. I told her about the party at David's—specifically Logan's behavior, my talk with Eric, and Logan's unexpected declaration. I also told her about all the days following. The hardest part, the part I needed to stop for several deep breaths during, was about the previous night.

As I talked, I watched Jetta's face express the same range of emotions that I had felt at the same moments I felt them. She didn't say anything, though—a bad sign from her. I finally ended with, "And now Logan hates me. He has to. How could he not?"

"I don't think he stopped loving you so quickly. There was only a five-day span between the party and yesterday."

I shrugged but had no vocal answer.

"So, Logan loved you, huh?" I watched as Jetta's mind replayed all the highlights of what I'd told her. "And the alcohol binge was—"

"Liquid courage? Apparently. By the way, after all your talk of how you noticed the way Eric looked at me, how did you never see the way Logan must have looked at me?"

She sighed. "Chrissie, do you think Logan watching you with love would look different than him watching you with affection?"

Huh. I hadn't thought about it that way.

"Are you sure it's over?"

"After last night? Oh, yes. It's over." I pretended the need to vomit in front of Robert, but I felt a real need to now. I closed my eyes and took a few slow breaths, willing those awful urges to go away.

"Well, I don't understand why he's being such a baby about it."

"What do you mean?" I asked, eyes still closed, hands on the edge of the sink behind me.

"So, you don't love him. Big deal."

"Jetta, I know you don't like Logan."

"This has nothing to do with that. Think about it. It's not like you two promised to one day fall madly in love with each other."

"Well, no, we didn't."

"Did he really need to break up with you because of that? Look at it this way: Couples stay together all the time and have less love between them than the two of you. Some people are coupled with each other for almost their entire adult lives and never love each other. He didn't give you the chance to develop those feelings."

"I had plenty of chances."

"How do you figure that?"

"We were together for nine months, not nine days. Nine months is long enough for it to go from cold and snowy to sweaty and hot back to cold again. It's long enough to know whether you love someone or not. Joe and Alissa have been together for less time than that and are madly in love. Time didn't matter to their relationship."

"Maybe you're right. Then again, maybe not. Every couple is different. You and Logan might have needed a longer time frame. Who's to say it wouldn't have happened eventually?"

I considered this. There was a part of me that wanted to love him—I mean *really* love him—when I thought about what not loving Logan did to him. But I couldn't. It was more than being scared. I couldn't do it.

I looked at Jetta again. "If it was going to happen, it would have already."

She stood at the sink next to me, quickly checking her hair in the mirror. "So, if you had done what I suggested?"

"What? Slept with him?"

She nodded.

"It still would have ended this way, only I'd feel a thousand times more nauseated right now."

She thought for a few seconds. "Well, you could always say it back. Tell Logan you love him. You don't have to mean it as long as he thinks you do."

I silently rolled my eyes.

"Chrissie, you know you could have said it."

"I would never lie to Logan like that."

"Don't think of it as lying. Think of it as telling him a future truth."

"Future truth?"

"Well, possible future truth. You can call him right now. Would you like me to get your phone?"

"No!" I put a hand out to stop her as she took a few steps toward the door.

She walked back. "Okay, you can do that later. It'll be an amazing surprise for him. Even an early Christmas present. He'll be grumbling through his day, missing the best woman he ever had. Then, all of a sudden, a phone call! It's her! She loves him! Best day ever!"

"That's so not funny. I am *not* calling him. Be serious."

"I am being—" she started before I gave a hard sigh and rolled my eyes again. "Okay, okay." She put her hands up. "I'm sorry. You really think he hates you?"

I nodded slowly.

Jetta took a moment to think. She also started fidgeting with her straightened hair again. Loops around one finger. Loops back the other way. Twisting and twisting. By the time she spoke again, almost every finger on one hand was wrapped with her black hair. "Chrissie, you don't love him. I doubt he hates you, but if he does, why do you care?"

I leaned my lower back against the sink I'd been holding on to. "I'm not sure if it's about that. I mean, obviously, I don't want him hating me."

"But you don't want him loving you, either, do you?" she asked slowly. "Be honest, Chrissie. How often did you ever actually think about Logan during the course of a day? At least, as of late. Did he cross your mind a lot? Did you wonder where he was and what he was doing, like you did about Eric?"

I slowly and sheepishly shook my head.

"Look, I'm no relationship expert, but even before this whole mess, you and Logan were not on a path to marriage."

"I know th—" I began before Jetta put a hand up.

"I'm not sure you understand. You and Logan know each other's families, yet you never attended family functions together. You never had meals with each other's parents."

I opened my mouth to speak again, but she stopped me.

"Despite the fact that you think it's a far drive to see either of your parents, you and I both know if you'd planned on marrying Logan at any point, you absolutely would have wanted him to spend time with your mom and dad. You would have pushed to see his, too. You can't tell me I'm wrong."

I couldn't tell her anything close to it. She was right.

"I just... I never wanted to hurt Logan. And it seems to be the only thing I've done to him."

That realization hit me hard. I had been so stupid about my entire relationship with Logan.

He was right. I was always the one to go on and on about how happy we were together without being bogged down by deep, penetrating feelings. I thought Logan felt the same. But the truth was that I couldn't remember a single occasion he'd agreed with me about it, even just a little. I'd forced what I wanted on him, and he cared too much about me to oppose me.

It explained all the time he spent away from me. Why fall madly in love with someone and subsequently want to spend every waking moment with them when that person has made it perfectly clear that's not close to what they want?

Maybe it didn't excuse Logan's inattention, but I definitely understood.

I was in a pretty understanding mood. After all, *I* was the biggest problem and ultimate downfall in our relationship. And if Logan had told me he loved me sooner, even before I met Eric, my reaction would have been exactly the same, as would my answer.

I remembered the conversation I had with Eric when I explained how Logan and I began. He'd called it "interesting," but I now knew it was a disaster waiting to happen. In over nine months' time, I hadn't been honest with anyone about my relationship, myself included. I'd always glossed over the things I didn't like or pretended those things didn't matter in the grand scheme of life.

I felt like such an idiot.

I began to tear up again in the bathroom. A few droplets left my eyes and slowly started trickling down my cheeks. I tried to stop them, though, because Jetta wasn't good with crying. Anytime someone cried—especially me— she was soon in tears as well.

To her credit, she did the best she could, considering we both knew at that moment, she wanted to sprint her desk in order to maintain her composure. She handed me a tissue and gave me a quick hug. "Are you going to be okay?"

I turned to face the mirror and dabbed at my eyes, trying hard not to smear my mascara. At least the clump was finally gone. "Yeah. I'll be fine." I nodded with a smile at her reflection. "I'm just being a total girl right now." That brief moment of crying did one other good thing. It put a little color back into my previously snow white complexion.

"Okay." She wiped at her now teary eyes and hugged me again. "I still love you."

"I love you, too."

She took a glance at her watch. "Chrissie, we need to get moving if we're going to be on time for our meeting. I don't want to deal with Mari's wrath today."

"Okay," I answered, thinking the wrath of Mari sounded much better than reliving the last few days anymore. Her yelling would absolutely deafen out any other thoughts for a while. But who *wanted* to hear their boss yell at them? I was already sad. I didn't want to be crazy, too. "Let's go."

We headed to Jetta's desk, where I grabbed my purse. I dropped it off at my own desk, along with the coat I still wore. I quickly adjusted my jacket and pants and checked my makeup one last time. Finally, I picked up the folders, notebook, laptop, and writing utensils I needed for the meeting.

Jetta and I didn't talk much on the way downstairs. I wasn't in the mood for conversation, and I knew she was terrified of making me cry again.

Honestly, I was afraid of that, too. At that moment, I was silently singing my favorite classic Rihanna song in my head in order to distract myself. It was a good part, too. It's the part I might have started dancing to if I was in a lighter mood.

I'm sure Jetta would have dropped her notebook and danced along with me if I'd asked her. We were alone in the elevator. But for some reason, I didn't say anything. I was feeling so much more than self-conscious. Jetta and I both knew that.

As the elevator passed through one floor, then the next, I remembered that Logan had no problem dancing no matter what his mood happened to be. He would dance any moves anyone could name, wherever he was, including stores and restaurants. The "sprinkler," the "shopping cart," anything. Dozens of moves that I didn't know the names of. With or without music. I'd witnessed him dance like that countless times when we were with friends.

In one of the funniest moments I had ever seen, Logan and Jetta performed the full routine of 'N SYNC's "Tearin' Up My Heart" in my apartment one lazy Saturday. It was goofy and unexpected and actually really good. I don't remember how it all started, the idea of dancing. Not initially, anyway. Jetta mentioned a 1990s version of "Pop-Up Video" she saw, which started the two of us on who was better: 'N SYNC or The Backstreet Boys. Who had better music? Who had better moves? In the end, neither won, but we had loads of fun getting to that conclusion.

When Logan mentioned that we could find their music videos online, we immediately went to YouTube. For an hour, we watched every video we could find. Jetta put herself in charge of choreography, and I took charge of the music. We moved all the furniture we could, enough to give them space to dance around and not run into anything. Eventually, all the dance moves, and corresponding body parts, were in sync, so to speak. Perfect synchronization.

Logan and Jetta tried convincing me to dance along with them. Logan even tried physically pulling me onto their little dance floor, but I held back, just as I did in the elevator.

As Jetta and I walked down the corridor, I recognized some of Eric's colleagues exiting a conference room. I slowed my pace to Eeyore's speed, hoping to catch a glimpse of him. He never came out, however, and when we reached the room, I noticed it was empty.

"He's not here," I accidentally whispered aloud. "But he never misses a meeting."

I looked over to see Jetta glancing from me into the empty room and back again. I instinctively put a hand to my mouth, but it was too late for that.

While I'd never intended for Jetta to hear me, I was grateful that she did. I knew that she knew exactly who I was talking about. Without needing to say a word to me, she casually grabbed Joe, who stood near us with one of his team members, and asked where Eric was. She made up some story about needing to talk to him because he was going to set her up with his friend and she had to change the day due to scheduling conflicts. I almost laughed at the way she explained it, but it proved good enough to get an answer.

Unfortunately, it *so* was not an answer I wanted to hear.

"Oh, he won't be coming here anymore."

Chapter Twenty-One

Jetta darted her eyes to me as she asked Joe, "What do you mean he won't be here?"

"Well, not for any meetings. Griff transferred to a different department."

"Are you sure?" Jetta and I asked at the same time. "Like, really sure?" she continued. "Maybe you're mistaken."

My heart pounded; my head spun. Joe had to be mistaken. He just had to.

Joe shook his head. "I'm positive. I don't know all the details, but for whatever reason, he won't be here again to work on our campaign for them. His co-workers said it all happened sometime yesterday."

Of course, it did. As if that day hadn't been cruel enough to me. As if it hadn't kicked me when I was down and laughed in my face. The two things I hated most about my life had to happen within the same twenty-four hours, didn't they?

"But it's so soon," I blurted without thought. The fear and then knowledge of Eric's absence shut down the sensible part of my brain. I couldn't focus on anything but him. I didn't even try.

I instantly regretted my blabber mouth, until Jetta added, "Yeah. I mean, don't things like that take time? I don't see how he could transfer so quickly. Especially since he was, like, head of the account or something, right?"

Super Bestie saves the day again!

"I don't know." Joe shrugged, adjusting the dress shirt I knew he bought specifically for working on Eric's campaign. No wearing band T-shirts to a meeting full of bankers. "It sucks, though, because he was a great guy to work with. He knew how to keep things focused but still fun. He wasn't uptight about anything. He let us do our jobs the way we needed to do them. Not what we were expecting out of someone from their company."

I knew this had to be true. Eric made everything fun.

"Even Markowitz and Galliano seemed to like him."

Wow! Impressing both agency partners was not an easy task. Not at all. Yet, Eric had done it. Why, oh why, did this amazing man have to disappear?

"Is she okay?" Joe asked, temporarily moving his dark-hued eyes my way.

"Oh, she's not feeling all that great," Jetta answered. She gave Joe a brief history of our made-up morning.

At some point, I no longer heard her. If I was white as snow before, I'm sure I was almost transparent at this point. All the blood had drained from me and evaporated into nothingness. Joe walked away, but my eyes didn't really see him. They were full of little dots and fuzzies. My breath was simultaneously speeding up and slowing down, a strange combination that had me near hyperventilation. I felt so weak that I almost dropped the meeting supplies I held in my hands. It was hard enough trying to prevent my laptop from slipping out of my arms.

I had to face it. Eric was gone. And I knew it was because of me. He had transferred out of his department and possibly even jeopardized his job to avoid seeing me. That gave me such an awful feeling inside. A horrendously sickening feeling.

At the same time, though, I couldn't blame him. He had made it clear how he felt about me. He told me he couldn't be around me. This sudden change was far from what I expected, however. I mean, I knew we wouldn't be hanging out anymore, but I honestly never thought he'd go as far as changing his job.

I'd missed being near him on quite a few occasions before, but that was nothing compared to how I felt in this moment. The hall, the conference room floor, the entire building felt so much emptier without Eric in it when he was supposed to be. This emptiness only re-emphasized how important he was to me. I needed him to come back. I wanted to return to our walks, return to times when it was just the two of us. When we talked openly and honestly like best friends about everything, even the awkward stuff. I would have paid a million dollars working as many jobs as it took to relive the baby discussion if it meant seeing him again.

I no longer had Logan. Now, I didn't have Eric.

Finally, I became aware of my surroundings again. I found Jetta standing near me, her hand resting comfortingly on my elbow. I leaned back slightly against the wall behind me, clutching my armful of stuff. *Breathe in. Breathe out. You have to keep it together.*

"I'm so sorry, Chrissie," Jetta whispered.

We watched the other member of our team—in other words, a very ticked off Robert—and some people from the art department walk past us toward the meeting room. Robert looked like he was about to say something to us. Like he wanted to give us an earful about how angry he was. Why weren't we in the conference room already? Why were we loitering in the hall? Blah blah blah. But the glare Jetta gave him was enough to send him silently on his way.

"It's okay." I managed a smile to Jetta. I had no idea how. I didn't even feel my mouth move. It was as numb as everything else. "Eric wasn't going to be around here forever. I'm sure he would have left at some point, anyway. I doubt he would have headed their team for all of time."

"Maybe it's not such a bad thing, though," Jetta said with a hopeful voice.

"What do you mean?" I took a deliberate breath in and let another one out.

I tried that old cliché of imagining my "happy place." The main problem I encountered was that I had no idea what my happy place was. I didn't even know what it was supposed to be. A favorite memory? A beloved person? A vast meadow of wildflowers near a softly babbling brook?

Since nothing special came to mind, I returned to the deep calming breaths. I was desperately hoping something would pull me away from the desire to curl into a ball on the floor and disappear for a while.

"Well, I don't know," Jetta continued. "But there has to be a reason for it to be a good thing. Maybe the bank has some company policy barring employees from dating each other."

"There's one big problem with that. I don't work for his company."

"No, but our company works for his. The no dating thing might extend into that."

"I highly doubt it." My body was still too weak for me to roll my eyes.

"It's possible," Jetta insisted. "You might not work for the same company, but he was here all the time. It was almost like you two were co-workers. Pretty damn close. Since he's now in a different department, he won't be here. The rule won't apply to him anymore. He's free to ask you out."

I shook my head at her, thinking how wrong she had to be about so much of that. There might have been hope for his happiness, but there was no hope left for us.

"He doesn't know I'm single, Jetta," I replied, almost choking on the word "single." It wasn't a word I'd used to describe myself in quite some time.

Jetta lowered her voice more as the art director breezed past us toward our designated conference room. "You don't think anyone would tell him about your breakup with Logan?"

"They wouldn't have any reason to. No one knows about anything between me and Eric."

Jetta nodded absently, but I knew she didn't believe me. She had always said that if she noticed the energy between Eric and me, everyone else must have as well. "I guess that lunch you and Eric planned definitely won't be happening now."

Oh, the lunch. I had so looked forward to our lunch date. That is, up until Eric walked away from me at the engagement party. This really was the final nail in the coffin on that.

"Joe's right," Jetta eventually sighed. "This sucks."

I couldn't describe it any better than that, so I stayed quiet.

"I guess that unknown guy we passed is Eric's replacement," she added.

"That's Ian. He's actually been here before. Several times." By now, I'd pulled myself away from the wall, praying that my legs wouldn't give out.

"Has he? I never saw him."

Very strange for her to not notice every man within a fifty yard radius, but I didn't mention this. I didn't think she would appreciate me pointing out how off her man radar had been.

After another second, she asked, "Um, so, how mad at me would you be if I said how cute Eric's possible replacement is?"

"Not mad, all things considered." I'd expected her to notice him eons before this moment. Now that she had finally seen him, of course she had to comment on him. "He is pretty hot."

"Pretty hot? He's so hot, he could melt a glacier just by looking at it."

Maybe he was, but I didn't care about that. "If you say so."

"If I say so? Have you looked at the man?"

"Okay, fine. He's sex on a stick. Better?"

"Better." Jetta grinned. Then the hair twirling began again.

"What's wrong?" I asked. I prayed it was nothing. I didn't think I could handle any more catastrophes.

"Oh, nothing. Not really. I was wondering if he's growing a sweater under the suit."

I rolled my eyes but also couldn't hold in a short laugh. "Come on. Almost everyone else is already in the meeting room. We're going to be late if we don't move. And Mari seems out for blood right now."

Chapter Twenty-Two

Through the days that followed, I gradually became more like myself again. I smiled more. I laughed every so often. Logan and I broke up days before Christmas, but I still had a decent holiday. Jetta and my family did their best to keep my mind otherwise engaged, lest any pesky "I want Logan here" thoughts popped up. I never told anyone when those ideas came to me. I actually embraced the loneliness. I'd assumed I would be completely consumed by it after Logan dumped me, but I was wrong. The loneliness became such a low, steady level that I began to not notice it. My job even started to improve. I was finally doing my work for real again—work so good that I loved turning it in to Mari.

Just over a week had passed when I started boxing up the things that reminded me of Logan. Souvenirs from baseball games, little mementos of shared favorite moments, the few presents he bestowed on me. Included in these were the ticket stubs to our first-date movie as well as the brochure from a lake resort in Wisconsin where we water-skied with friends one weekend in July. I also added every picture he and I ever took together, including the one I'd used as my computer background photo. I printed it out and deleted it from my laptop.

I also packed away my Ryne Sandberg jersey. Logan hadn't given it to me; I bought it off eBay before we started dating. It had to go away, though. It held too many memories of time spent with Logan. Too many moments of wearing the jersey while he held me in his arms. Logan had often told me how much he loved seeing me in the jersey—a fitted style one, not bulky or boxy. It was always a sight he said turned him on more than most of my other clothes. Once, when I wore the jersey with short shorts and wedges, I thought Logan was going to lose his mind. That or his eyeballs, considering how much they almost popped out of their sockets.

I sealed up the small shoebox of stuff and placed it on a shelf in my closet, unsure where it would end up in the future but also certain I needed it out of sight for the time being.

I'd done that with stuff from my previous boyfriends, too. However, after running into one of them, one with whom I definitely did not have an amicable split, I destroyed all those mementos in a fit of frustration. Everything I couldn't burn in my fireplace got tossed in the garbage then pitched into a dumpster.

Of course, I regretted doing this after the fact. Once it was too late to get any of it back. I didn't see me throwing the box away this time around. Without knowing exactly how or when, I knew there would come a point in time when remembering Logan wouldn't hurt anymore. When thinking of him would bring a smile to my face.

On a bitterly cold Sunday evening soon after New Year's, I was busy mapping out dialogue for a commercial script when there was a knock at my door. I hadn't been expecting anyone and was startled enough that I jumped at the sound. After standing, I glanced down at my faded gray yoga pants, stained pink sweatshirt, and fuzzy slippers with chagrin, wishing I looked more presentable. Not that it mattered, but I felt a little self-conscious. I contemplated at least changing my clothes, wondering if whoever it was would wait that long.

After a second or two, though, I gave up the debate and answered the door.

"Logan! Hi!" I smiled, unable to move anything but my mouth. My hand gripped the doorknob; my feet felt cemented to the tile. The only other willingly active body part was my heart. It banged around in my chest to the point where I thought it might give out from exhaustion.

"Hi." He grinned in return.

I couldn't even begin to understand how sexy he looked. Perfect hair, perfect smile. He wore a thick, unzipped coat over what appeared to be his—and my—favorite green sweater. For some reason, even his dark wash jeans seemed to fit his body better than ever.

Something inside me quivered as he leaned one arm against the doorframe. "I was hoping you'd be home."

"Well, you found me." The smile was plastered on my face, but inside, I felt more shock than anything. I hadn't seen him in almost two weeks. Honestly, I wasn't sure I'd ever see him again. I figured I was his least favorite person.

None of our mutual friends had said anything to me about the breakup beyond how sorry they were, Jesse included. That didn't mean that Logan wasn't already badmouthing me, however. He very well could have hated me at this point. Yet, there he stood in my doorway, actually giving me a smile, of all things.

He moved his eyes into the apartment then back to me. "May I?"

"Oh! Yes. Please come in." I stepped aside, feeling a little foolish for not inviting him in sooner. Luckily, I knew Logan didn't care that my place was in desperate need of a cleaning.

After he walked in, I shut the door behind him, wondering what in the world could have brought him there. Whatever it was, it made me happy to see him again. His presence seemed like a good sign.

While I knew he must have had a purpose for being at my apartment, he didn't say anything once inside. But then, neither did I. At the moment, I was having difficulty forming words in my head, let alone in my mouth. Logan remained by the door as I stood a few feet in front of him. I fidgeted with a sweatshirt string; he shuffled his feet. I crossed one leg in front of the other and moved it back. Logan shifted his weight from his left side to his right.

We each stared in the other's direction in awkward silence for another moment or two before I asked, "So, how have you been?"

It was a stupid, insensitive question. Of course, I knew his feelings during those days and weeks. Most of them were probably downright awful. My question was the first thing that came to mind, and really, it was a normal question to ask a person one hasn't seen in a while.

Logan flinched ever-so-slightly and shrugged. "Oh, you know. I've been better."

I bit the inside of my lip. "I know. I'm sorry."

As I watched him, I realized we had come to a moment when I normally would have hugged or kissed him, maybe rubbed his cheek. Anything to see him smile again. But I knew there was nothing I could do this time. I had done enough.

He shrugged again with a nod, silently telling me he didn't want to talk about it anymore.

This was typically the moment when my mouth would override my brain's decision to give him the peace he desired. It was the moment I would talk on and on about exactly how sorry I felt. I would have unloaded all my guilt and probably unintentionally added to his pain.

I realized something, though, as I looked into Logan's face. There *was* a way to help him. I simply had to give him what he desired. I had to drop the subject. There was only one problem with that. I didn't know what else to say.

Logan took the hint. "I was looking for a few of my movies today and realized you have them. That's actually why I'm here."

"Of course." I smiled. "I'll get them for you."

As I walked to the entertainment center, I noticed that Logan stayed where he was. If we were still a couple, fighting or not, he would have followed me into the living room. This was a sure sign to me that we were definitely over.

Without wanting to think about it, I searched my randomized disc collection for Logan's movies, finding them fairly quickly. As I looked, my eyes caught sight of the movie I bought for our doomed last day. This was the first time I was honestly happy I hadn't left it in my garbage can. I was also happy I never put it in the box with the other mementos. It was something that could serve as a sort of connection with Logan, whether or not he knew it.

Movies in hand, I turned to him again. His eyes were looking at our first-date flick. As I watched him, I think he realized what had also occurred to me about that particular film. He moved his gaze to me and gave a brief sort of smile.

I silently returned to the foyer to hand him his movies. He took them from me with yet another grin and a thanks before turning to leave. After a step, he stopped. He slowly moved his body around to face me again.

"Is there anything else you want?" I asked a little nervously, honestly hoping he'd say no. "It's all boxed up now, but—"

"No," he answered quickly with a headshake.

I'd mostly avoided his eyes until this point. I was afraid of what I might see. I figured that after having been around me for a few minutes, his eyes were bound to give something away. I didn't think I wanted to know what it was. But as he caught my gaze, I realized there wasn't much to fear.

I'd expected hate or anger or even disgust, but what I saw was what they usually showed. He was hurting, yes, but there was also a little friendship still in his eyes. The love was there, too, just a bit altered. It wasn't as deep and intense as before. I suspected it would lessen even more as time passed on. Seeing the expression in his eyes was bittersweet yet heartening at the same time.

"Anything I gave you was a gift. That's all yours to keep or do whatever you want with." He shrugged.

"I'd like to keep everything." It was in this very moment I decided I wanted to keep all of it from him, for always. I added slowly, "I'd like to think you want to keep your stuff, too."

He sighed, but it wasn't really an annoyed one. "Of course I do. It isn't like I want to pretend we didn't exist, Christabel. We had a relationship. I don't want to forget that."

"I know. I don't want that, either. I'm *so* sorry, Logan," I whispered, choking back a sudden thickness in my throat. "I'm sorry for having been selfish and aloof. I'm sorry for so many things. I know that probably doesn't mean much to you right now."

"It helps."

He sighed again and rubbed his face for a few moments. Then he gazed at me again. "Look, I know this all sucks, but I'm sure you'll get over me in no time."

"Why would you say that?" I asked.

"Come on. I know about you and Griff."

My heart dropped with a thud. "What?" I squeaked through my shock.

"I'm not an idiot, Christabel. I've seen you two look at each other."

Oh shit, I thought. How had I been so stupid?

I shook my head. "This isn't about Eric, Logan."

It really wasn't. This was about what Logan and I felt for each other in the wake of our breakup. It was about healing ourselves and each other, even if we reassembled one broken piece out of a million.

"And you're wrong about me getting over you."

Surprise took over his face. "Am I?"

I grinned. "You're a lot harder to forget than you might think."

He smiled in return and left.

I thought about him once he was gone. Neither of us had bothered to buy a Christmas present for the other. I knew him well enough to know that if he'd bought me something, he would have said so.

Before the holiday, I had a whole slew of perfectly chosen presents in the corner next to my tiny tabletop Christmas tree. Each gift was carefully wrapped in metallic blue snowflake paper and adorned with hand-tied silk ribbons. I had a different color ribbon for each person. None of them were for my boyfriend. Not one. He had been number one on my shopping list, but I didn't even have gift ideas written next to his name. In hindsight, I could list off a dozen or more things Logan would have loved. Back then, however, my mind was completely blank—a fact that hadn't fazed me all that much.

It was confusing how I had cared about Logan and also not cared at the same time. He deserved better than thoughtless indifference. He deserved a happiness that I could not give him or share with him.

Logan held the ability to be a great boyfriend to someone. I hoped he would find her. As for me, I wasn't sure who I could be that woman for, if even for anyone.

Jetta was determined that I should be with Eric, something she argued with me about one day, three weeks after Logan dumped me. It was a rare free day for both of us, and we decided to make the most of it: manicures, pedicures, a long leisurely lunch, and the ever-important recreational shoe-shopping.

"It's been too long," she told me while standing in DSW. "You need to call Eric."

Without answering, I returned a pair of knee-high fur-trimmed boots to the display in front of me. Nothing in the aisle inspired me, so I moved on to strappy sandals.

Jetta followed me, refusing to give up. "Seriously, Chrissie. I don't understand why you won't call him."

In the next aisle, I reached for a red patent-leather stiletto from the shelf, admiring the detailed straps. I knew it would look fabulous with my navy and white polka dot dress. I already owned a belt that coordinated with the shoes perfectly. Finally, I turned to face her. "Because, Jetta. First of all, think of what a slap in the face that would be to Logan. It would be like proving he was right, that I did get over him in an instant and went straight to Eric's arms. I don't want to do that."

I looked around, finding the red heel in my size, along with Jetta's. I pulled the boxes off the shelf, handing her size to her. We sat down to try on the shoes, me on the bench and Jetta on the floor.

"I'm sure Logan's already getting over you."

I shrugged. "I don't know. Maybe he is."

"He might be over you by now. Like, completely over you. Even if he isn't, he's on the path to it. No doubt he's dating other women now. He'd want some sexy new flings to make him forget all about you. Which means he neither hates nor loves you."

"Can we not talk about this please?" I implored as I finished buckling up the straps. Out of the corner of my eye, I saw Jetta stop what she was doing.

"Be honest, Chrissie. How does it make you feel to imagine Logan dating other women?"

I took a breath and let it out. In my mind, I could see Logan holding a woman in his arms. He kissed her forehead and her lips. He gave her a tight hug. He was happy.

I turned to Jetta. "I feel happy for him."

"Good." she smiled. "That's progress. Now, don't you think Logan would feel the same for you? He won't care about you dating someone else, even Eric. Who is going to tell Logan, anyway? No one, that's who." She brushed her newly-dyed fiery red hair behind her left shoulder and stood.

"Eric made it perfectly clear that he doesn't want to be around me anymore."

Standing, I turned to Jetta, who was admiring the heels in a small floor-adjacent mirror. "Yeah, but that's because you were with Logan. You aren't with him now. I'm sure Eric would love to hear from you. That I would absolutely guarantee."

"You don't know that. I don't know that. No one knows but Eric, and he's not telling. Can we just leave it at that?" Jetta and I silently switched back to our own shoes, then we started for the checkout.

Jetta spoke again as we waited in line. "You're right. We don't know what Eric wants or what he thinks. But the only way to find out is to call him."

"I can't do that."

I began carefully examining the red heels I held. Both shoes were the same size, something I always checked after once buying what turned out to be a left 8 and a right 9.

Jetta snapped her fingers in my face to catch my attention.

"What?"

"Chrissie, you can call him. You have to."

"No, I don't have to. And you're not getting it."

"You have his number."

"Yes. But I *can't*."

"Of course, you can. It's easy. I'll show you." She pulled her cell out of her purse. "You simply dial the numbers and press send. Just like so..." she said as she pushed the buttons on the screen.

A few seconds later, my phone began to ring.

"Well, what do you know? Your phone works, too! Since it's already on, you might as well call him now."

"Will you please drop the subject?" I sighed.

Jetta put her hands on her hips. "So, after everything you two felt and I'm sure still feel for each other, you're going to give up on him? You're not going to try, even once? See if he still feels the same?"

"I don't see what good it would do." Despite every effort to sound strong, my voice came out small and a little defeated.

"I cannot believe I'm hearing this. Are you kidding me right now?"

It was our turn with the cashier. He quickly rang up my stilettos then Jetta's choices. We paid for our purchases, headed out, and got in the car.

"That was fun," Jetta said. "So, back to Eric." She grinned, clasping her seatbelt buckle.

I tossed our bags into the back seat. "Look, whatever happened with Eric doesn't matter now. He chose to remove me from his life—"

"Technically, he removed himself from your life," Jetta interrupted, turning the key in the ignition. "That's what he told you, remember? And I'm sure he thought he didn't have a choice. He did what he thought was best."

I listened to her but didn't reply.

Truth was, while I didn't miss Logan, I felt an immense, unrelenting emptiness inside without Eric around.

I sighed as Jetta began pulling out of the parking lot. "I'm not going to force myself on Eric. I refuse to be that kind of woman. I'm no stranger to being alone. It's not like I've never been single before. I'll be fine."

Chapter Twenty-Three

It had been three months since I last saw Eric. He never returned to the agency. I didn't know how much he hung out with David, Loretta, and all them. No one mentioned him to me.

Jetta felt the same as she did three months before, but she'd somehow learned to stay away from that topic. At least to me. I knew she thought about it even though she tried to deny it. There was no way it was easy for her to avoid discussing Eric with me, so I definitely admired her for that.

I had been trying to remind myself how imperfect Eric actually was. For starters, he had a very messy car. Loose change, straw wrappers, randomly displaced rocks, and spots of dirt. The only thing missing was the bad smell. He also hated combing his hair. He was lucky if he could remember where his comb was. He had a severe distaste of any food that had the word "salad" in its description, no matter how delicious. And he really, *really* hated greeting cards. He said they were pointless. Especially "just because" ones, like, "This is just because I am thinking of you." He said it was much better to call the person or visit them than send a stupid card.

"Cards are such a waste of money," he'd ranted one day. "They cost a fortune, considering they're made out of paper, not gold or silver. Besides, they end up being immediately thrown away ninety-nine times out of a hundred." He refused to listen to all the wonderful points of both giving and receiving well-written greeting cards.

And... that was as far as I ever got. I occasionally started along the lines of, "I really hate the way he..." or "It's so annoying how he..."

It never went further than that. There were way too many things I liked about Eric to focus on the "bad" stuff.

I had a feeling Jetta filled Alissa, and in extension Joe, in on the general basics of the "Eric and Christabel story." Every so often, I caught them looking at me with a certain similar expression on their faces. Especially Alissa. I couldn't be around her because I couldn't handle the unwanted, though usually silent, sympathy. And even though she was quiet, Jetta always managed to send sad little smiles my way at work.

I was surprised she hadn't just called Eric for me, but maybe she had and he wasn't interested after all. The negative side of myself would at least be pleased about being right. It hurt too much to contemplate how the rest of me would feel having that kind of knowledge.

It wasn't typical of all our clients, or even most of them, but Eric's company decided to throw a party for the entire ad agency as a thank you for our collective hard work on their campaign. The overhaul was already a huge success, and it hadn't even been a week since the new brand was unveiled.

We were in the Grand Ballroom of the Washington Hotel on Michigan Avenue. It was a fabulous room, with gigantic crystal chandeliers, marble columns, and views of the Chicago River. There were fancy food stations everywhere complete with pasta dishes, fresh sushi, and carved beef. Waiters in sharp, black tuxedos were carrying around silver trays of smaller hors d'oeuvres and glasses of champagne. A jazz band—well, orchestra—was playing for our listening pleasure. Everything and everyone in here seemed to glisten or sparkle in some way. Fabulous dresses, snazzy suits. It was like we were living out a scene in a movie.

We had the entire ballroom to ourselves, and it was definitely well-filled. Almost every employee of both companies was there, including the agency's partners and the bank's CEO.

Everyone except Eric.

I hadn't seen him around. Neither had anyone else, according to Jetta. She asked Joe and another guy on his team to stay on alert, but it didn't seem to be necessary. What it seemed like was an immense mortification. I couldn't believe any colleagues other than Jetta knew about any of that. She promised she didn't tell anyone why they needed to look for Eric, just that she would appreciate it. I doubted anyone believed that, though. I didn't want to know how badly the story was going to be twisted around by the end of the night.

Even though my entire company was at the party, I was pretty much by myself. I didn't recognize anyone around me. Most of my close colleagues had disappeared, including

Jetta, who was probably having sex in the coatroom. She took off with Ian, Eric's replacement on the campaign. Actually, she'd been dating Ian for the last two months or so, against the rule I felt so bound by.

I didn't have a date for the gala. I hadn't dated since Logan. At all.

A month ago, before Jetta's twenty-eighth birthday blowout, she set up four potential dates for me. I had no desire to meet any of them, but she called it a payback of the favor I promised her months earlier. I contended I'd already fulfilled that favor.

How was this for a bad sign? Four potential dates, and I still ended up solo at the party.

Okay, well, to be completely honest with myself, it was my fault. Not in that "I didn't deserve them" kind of way. I was sure they were great guys. I also knew that I was pretty fabulous to have as a girlfriend, or I could be if I put forth the effort. But I totally sabotaged myself. Each man and I did the whole "getting to know each other by text" thing first before I would agree to meet. I somehow managed to divulge to all four of them everything that happened in the drama with Eric, Logan, and me.

They ran away pretty fast after that.

My dear best friend was informed of this by at least two of them and was quick to tell me how crazy I was making myself seem. "Guys are going to walk away from you thinking you're either insane or desperate."

"I am not crazy. I'm not insane, nor am I desperate. I was never going to find what I wanted with those guys."

Jetta was disappointed for me—the only one of us to feel this way. None of those four had the kind of qualities I wanted them to possess. Not even close. No matter how perfect they might otherwise have been, there was one trait in particular none of them could ever have. One thing none of them could ever be. Besides, despite my friend's best efforts to land me a date, I had a fantastic time at Jetta's b-day party all by myself.

I was not in a hurry to find a man. I knew what I wanted from someone, what I was willing to compromise on, and what would make me run away screaming. Both Logan and Eric played a part in shaping these thoughts, and maybe not even how someone else might think.

I wanted to find the *right* guy, or really, to have the right guy find me. And I knew people said it happens when you least expect it, but a little forewarning would be nice. Just a small whisper, like, "Hey, Christabel, that man in the brown jacket over there is your perfect guy." Was that asking for too much?

For two weeks before the grand company celebration, Jetta pushed me as much as she could about finding a date. She told me every reason she could think of, mainly two major points:

1) "You should never go to a work function alone."
2) "Having a date for the party could lead to a new relationship."

Jetta reasoned every motive except the one I knew she was silently thinking: "Going alone will make you look pathetic."

She even seriously suggested Logan several times.

I had hung out with Logan occasionally since our breakup.

It certainly wasn't easy in the beginning. Despite our calm encounter in my apartment, we were very glad to be away from each other. Things were too raw to make seeing one another anything but unbearable. Then a mutual friend of ours from high school held a "reunion" party of sorts at her house. I knew Logan might attend but took the risk, anyway.

Left alone once for several minutes, he and I awkwardly chatted about my work, his new job... really simple topics. Nothing too deep or personal. No more sharing secrets for us. He also showed me his brand new tattoo—something he never would have gotten if we were still together. He admitted that when he lifted the bandage off his arm for me to see the ink.

Logan told me he had wanted one for a while but didn't want to risk me hating it, which I absolutely would have. I admitted that to him as I at least attempted to admire the tattoo.

Somehow, the encounter encouraged us enough to want to see each other again. As time moved on, we developed, or perhaps returned to, a fantastic harmony of friendliness. I even gave him a quick hug the last time I saw him. It was reciprocated with enough sweetness to tell me that we were, and would be, okay.

It seemed clearing up the whole "I love you" thing, even with the subsequent fight and breakup, released the pressure that had been building between us for quite a while. That clarity helped Logan see our relationship from my point of view. It made him stop blaming me as much as he had.

Who knew, right? Certainly not me. And not Logan, either, as far as I could tell. Neither one of us expected this.

During one of our chance encounters, I mentioned this very party to him. He and I visibly recognized the moment I would have normally asked him to come with me. I didn't, though. I didn't think it would be right. He was sweet enough to offer me his companionship for the evening, but I declined.

Before Jetta disappeared, she'd told me again how much she wished I'd taken Logan up on his offer. A few hours before the soirée began, she left a message on my phone telling me how easy it would be for me to invite Logan. She was convinced bringing him would be better than bringing no one.

I wasn't so sure.

At that moment, we were about two weeks away from what would have been our technical one-year anniversary. It was the beautiful day I wanted to recreate when we broke up. I didn't know if Logan remembered the anniversary, but it was one reason I didn't accept the offer.

I had shaken my head at Jetta in reply. "Jetta, Logan didn't mean it. He said it to be nice."

She nodded slightly, but I didn't think it was because of what I said. She looked lost in her thoughts, quietly sipping her champagne. After a moment, she said, "Chrissie, if I tell you something, will you be mad at me?"

"That depends, I suppose."

She looked nervous, which made me even more so.

"What is it? Do I need to sit down for this?" I laughed, attempting to add some levity to what was beginning to feel like a serious conversation.

She shared some sort of knowing glance with Ian, who had been hanging around nearby. He simply shrugged, and

Jetta looked back to me. "Okay, I'll just tell you. I called Logan yesterday."

"You-you what?" I stuttered. "But how... I mean, how did you... *Why?*"

If she was going to call anyone on my behalf, why Logan?

Her face scrunched as she replied in rapid succession. "I'm sorry, but I felt bad for you. I didn't want you here alone. And, honestly, he sounded so sweet about it. I apologized for what I was doing and for it being so last minute. He said he wasn't sure what he was doing tonight, if he had any plans he couldn't remember, but he could try to make it if you really wanted him to."

Jetta and I might have disagreed now and then, but I didn't think she'd ever upset me as much as she did with this. I felt a swell of anger that burst out of me. "*Jetta!* I can't believe you did that! Are you insane?"

She ignored my last question. "Logan doesn't think you're desperate or pathetic or anything. I explained to him that it was my doing, not yours. But I also said you do like being around him again, which is true."

I had to nod reluctantly at that one.

"And you still care about each other. That much hasn't changed."

"No, it hasn't." I shook my head slightly. I momentarily rubbed my temples with a heavy sigh. "I cannot believe you called him."

"I know," she answered sheepishly.

I closed my eyes and tried some deep breathing, but that didn't take away the anger. All I could do was remind myself that she called Logan out of concern for me and ignore the part of me that kept thinking what a crap-filled mess everything was. "I am *so* angry with you right now!"

"I know that, too." She genuinely sounded sorry, but for which part, I couldn't tell. I guessed it was less about what she did and more for the simple fact that I was bothered by it.

I rubbed my forehead a moment. "But I don't miss *him*!" Once I closed my lips, I realized I'd emphasized one word in my mind and another with my mouth.

Ian spoke up. "I'm still team Griff. I told Jetta it was a bad idea to call your ex."

Jetta rolled her eyes and looked at me. "Maybe it isn't as bad as you think. I want Eric here, too, but you forbade me from contacting him. Besides, if he was interested in seeing you, wouldn't he be here by now?"

Neither Ian nor I had an answer.

I sighed again, refocusing on Jetta's face. "Do you think Logan is going to show up?"

"Don't know." She shrugged. "He might. I told him how to get in."

"Won't it be strange for us to be together tonight considering what's coming up?"

"If he can handle it, you can. Right?"

Right. Of course. Absolute piece of cake. Not!

She noticed the worry on my face and laughed. "Oh, Chrissie! Don't stress about it, okay? If you ever do fall in love with him someday, you'll thank me for this."

I wasn't sure about that. I thought it was an awful idea.

So, that was the main thought in my mind. I tried calling Logan, but it went straight to voice mail. I didn't know what to say so I didn't leave a message. I hadn't sent any texts, either.

I wanted to leave for the safety of home, but it seemed a little early to do so. Of course, there was also the fact that I hated the thought of leaving if Logan really was going to show up. It would have been bad enough being stood up, but to be stood up by your ex-girlfriend at her work party less than two weeks before what was supposed to be your first anniversary sounded just horrible. I couldn't do that to him.

I wandered around aimlessly, absently fingering the skirt of my black and gray tulle halter dress. I ate a little earlier so I wasn't hungry, and while I enjoyed the beautiful jazz the band was playing, I had no one to dance with. It made me wish they'd play something a little less romantic right now.

Jetta's voice was playing in my head along with the current Glen Miller tune. *"Do you still want to be with Eric? Or someone else? Do you want Logan again?"*

I started thinking about the man who I hoped would stroll through the door and guide me out onto the dance floor. But he wasn't there and would probably not show up.

Then I thought that maybe I should leave. I didn't care if my bosses noticed my early absence even though this was my last event with Madison.

In two weeks, I would be joining another local agency as a higher level copywriter. The agency was one of Chicago's top three, and also one of Madison's fiercest competitors. My new job wasn't a creative director spot, but it was a major step up. It also included a pay raise, but that was only a tiny part of why I applied for it.

I was up against a lot of competition for the job, but I knew I would come out on top. It didn't hurt that I had a strong, impressive portfolio. I also had a few advertising awards to throw in for good measure.

I loved my new creative team, my directors, everyone. It was exactly the atmosphere that Madison used to have. They had libraries, a movie room, and even a gym in their building. Almost anything and everything a creative could desire for a change of pace and peace of mind to jump-start their ideas when stuck with writer's block. Everything that was taken away from us at Madison was present, and even better than I knew it could be. On top of everything else, I would be able to travel to New York for meetings with some of our clients out there. Not on a once or twice a year basis, either.

Jetta desperately wanted a position at my new agency. I had to remind her every day for weeks that she would still have Alissa to talk to when I left. Of course, I was going to miss Jetta. I'd miss almost everyone, but I had to do what felt right. Just like Jetta was always pushing me to do. Even if it meant going out on my own.

While I was perfectly happy to go it alone in my career, I couldn't say the same relationship-wise. I thought I could handle it, but watching everyone else in the room, I felt so lonely. Like I was the only single person there. There was only one person who could put those feelings to rest.

I called Logan again and, as casually as I could, explained that the party was a bore and I was going home. I also apologized for my—well, frankly, Jetta's—intrusion into his weekend. As I ended the call, I really, *really* hoped I left the message in enough time.

After putting my phone back in my purse, I turned around to head for the coatroom. As I did so, I nearly ran into a very handsome man dressed in a sleek, dark gray suit, holding out a glass of champagne to me.

Chapter Twenty-Four

Oh. My. Word. Someone needed to call the folks at *People* magazine and tell them their search was over. I found the Sexiest Man Alive. He was standing right in front of me. Without a doubt, this was the hottest he had ever looked.

"Let me guess. I had 'champagne eyes,'" I said with a small grin, accepting the glass from Eric's extended hand. I took a sip as he gave a half -smile. My drink was bubbly, but it gave me no pleasure. The only pleasure I enjoyed was that of having Eric in front of me. I felt like nothing else could make me happy.

"You just looked like you could use it." He shrugged.

I watched him sip his own champagne and subsequently cringe. He was a beer guy, not a champagne guy, which made me wonder why he was even drinking it. Maybe he needed it as much as he thought I needed mine. I could only hope this wasn't because he wasn't happy to see me. He faced me, but his eyes were focused on the room around us.

My eyes, meanwhile, were focused on nothing but him. Without moving, I examined him more carefully, trying to take in as much of him as I could for later remembrances. I realized that his eyes were lacking every sort of brightness—a sad thing to see. His face was taut and lacked emotion, but it was as handsome as ever. Even without any vibrancy, he'd still look right at home on a magazine cover. He certainly lived up to all my memories of him. His gray silk tie was similar to the one he wore when we first met, I couldn't help noticing. I also couldn't help noticing how perfectly we coordinated with each other. I was pretty sure he didn't realize this, though.

I felt that familiar ache again. That desire to keep him near me for as long as possible. "I didn't think you were here," I told him. "No one has seen you around." Which hopefully told him that, yes, I had been paying attention. That I cared.

"I hadn't planned on coming, but some of the guys from your agency, Joe Fuller especially, asked me to. Joe said I helped a lot with the project and deserved the celebration for it. I figured it couldn't hurt to show up for a little bit. Sort of a last-minute decision."

Good old Joe. I loved Joe! If he was around, I would have kissed him. Actually, if *Jetta* was around, I would have kissed *her* since, I know it had to have been her idea. I was sure Joe probably would have asked Eric to come, anyway, but he wouldn't have pushed it as much without Jetta's influence. She had a way of getting what she wanted from people, I adored that about her.

I smiled again. "Well, I'm glad you changed your mind. It's really nice to see you."

Eric made no answer. He merely sipped his champagne.

"So, how do you like your new department?"

"It's okay. Different than what I was doing."

I nodded, my meticulously coifed loose curls bouncing with the movement. Because I couldn't help myself, I added, "Do you ever miss your old job?"

Of course, I wanted to ask him if he missed me, but I didn't dare.

I couldn't quite gauge his emotions as he shrugged. "Sometimes, I suppose. I mean, I didn't get a promotion out of it. It was more of a lateral move. But I like it."

"Good." I smiled. "You know, I'm actually starting a new job soon."

"Are you?" he asked, but he didn't seem all that interested in an answer. It made me wonder why he bothered coming over to me if he wasn't in the mood for conversation.

Little did he know that I was not about to give up so easily. I answered him despite his lack of enthusiasm. "Yep. I'm still a copywriter, only now I'm a higher level one." I lowered my voice to a decibel that only Eric could hear. "Their CD is supposed to be the best in the city. The best in the Great Lakes area, honestly. I think he might even be better than Georgina, the director Mari replaced, which is high praise, indeed." I gave a small, excited grin.

"That's nice." Two whole words; zero enthusiasm.

I was about to start some nervous rambling but bit my lip instead. No matter what I said, it wouldn't change his mind about me. Babbling on about anything would only annoy him at best and chase him away at worst.

At least my silence didn't scare him off. Though we weren't talking, he was close enough to touch without having to reach too far. Not that I was going to try, but I so wanted to.

Eventually, Eric said, "Pretty big crowd." Of course, he noticed this. He'd been watching the other people in the room more than anything else.

I took a glance around us. "Yeah. Should be for two entire companies." I paused, staring down at my hot pink heels. One hand held my barely drunk glass of champagne, the other my black satin clutch.

My heartbeats were rapidly increasing, as was the quickness of my breath. The pounding of my heart was even louder than our beautiful background music. I didn't' know what to do in this moment. Everything I had the urge to do didn't seem appropriate, given our history. Neither did anything I had the urge to say. I wanted to tell him a million things but one more than any other.

Finally, I came to a decision. Appropriate or not, I *had* to say it.

I raised my eyes to him again. "I've really missed you."

Eric's face remained expressionless, his voice silent.

I didn't know what I expected, but it didn't look like he felt the same. All that time I spent wondering about him and what, if anything, I still meant to him felt like such a waste.

I wished I had a way of knowing what he was thinking, but then, maybe I didn't. I wondered if he made a similar list about me that I made about him. Did he find a lot to dislike about me? What were my faults that he hated the most? Maybe I seriously didn't need to know.

At that moment, it looked like Eric wouldn't be telling me much of anything. After six months, we were almost back where we started.

The urge to run began to fill me again. I planted my feet as firmly to the floor as I could, however. I had to. I rejected the idea of giving up at least some sort of friendship with him, even if it was only for the next few minutes.

Keeping my voice as light as I could, I asked, "So, where's your date?"

"My what?"

Finally! A tiny, little hint of emotion. Utter surprise to be exact. I couldn't imagine why he was so surprised at that question, but I considered his reaction to be a major success.

"Your date. You know, the gorgeous, leggy woman who jumped at the chance to spend the evening with you."

He shrugged again but didn't look at me. "Don't have one."

"Oh, come on. A great catch like you without a date? What woman wouldn't want to be with you? She'd have to be crazy."

My tone was friendly and playful, but inside, I wanted to cry. I couldn't believe I was talking to him about dates. I knew it should be me; I should've been his date. The thought of him with other women started to eat at my resolve, but I refused to let it show.

Instead of answering me, Eric asked, "Where's your boyfriend?" His tone wasn't angry or even derisive. It was as blank as his face.

I kept my eyes glued on him as I shrugged. "I don't have one."

Eric's gaze, which had pretty much avoided me, darted to my face, focusing on my eyes. However, his voice was calm. "You did. What happened?"

I didn't know how many particulars to give him. I was pretty sure he had no desire to hear every gory detail about the demise of Logan and me. Some things really were better left unsaid. Whether I told him all or none of the details, there was only one part of it that mattered. I shrugged again. "He broke up with me a few months ago."

Eric started to nod, then I quickly added, "We didn't belong together. He isn't the one I want."

Our eyes locked again, and Eric looked earnestly at me. I had no idea what was going on in his head, but he appeared to be silently debating something.

My anxiety grew larger and larger inside me, like a giant monster that was trapped inside and trying fervently to get out. It gnawed at my body; it gnawed at my strength. What if I was right? What if it was too late? What if Eric didn't care anymore?

As my body weakened, I was glad I didn't wear higher heels. I would probably be on the floor. My legs were already teetering below me. It was also a good thing I hadn't finished my drink. I definitely didn't need anything else to add to my lightheadedness.

Eventually, Eric took my glass of champagne, giving both glasses to a passing waiter with an empty tray. He held his hand out to me. "Dance with me?"

I was so shocked I didn't move right away. I couldn't feel anything except my still-banging heart. Was I living in a movie? Was this all a dream? If it was, I didn't want to wake up. *Please, please don't let me wake up!*

Eric took a step nearer, giving my eyes a better look at his beautiful face. It was happy and relaxed, the way I was used to seeing him. The way I loved seeing him. Somehow, everything began functioning again.

This was not a dream. Eric didn't hate me. After all those months, I still meant something to him.

"No one else is dancing," I said stupidly. All the other dancing couples had disappeared back into the crowd.

"Do you care?" Eric asked with a twinkle in his eyes.

"No." I shook my head. "I really don't."

"So, will you dance with me?"

I was about to answer when he added with a sly grin, "As a sort of celebration."

"A celebration of what?" I asked as he took my free hand.

He moved closer to me, giving my hand a squeeze. It was the same kind of squeeze he gave me months before during our walk in the dark. The tingles in my hand rapidly spread through the rest of me, warming everything to the most perfect degree.

His voice was soft as he replied, "Our first day together."

If it were physically possible, I would have been a puddle. Those four words melted away all my fears, my apprehensions, my negativity, everything.

I beamed at him, feeling a happiness that had never filled me before. It was better than floating on a cloud. It was better than waltzing with Prince Charming on a rainbow. It was like a million birthdays, Christmases, work promotions, and first kisses all rolled into one incredible gift. I had no idea anything could feel like this.

Before I knew it, we were both leaning into the other. Eric's lips gently reached mine. Our slightly parted mouths caressed against each other, slowly at first, then with an earnestness that curled my fingers and toes. I had to consciously release my fingers from their grip on Eric's suit jacket in order to put a bit of distance between us. He grinned at me, clearly knowing it would be inappropriate to make out in front of his bosses but wanting to, anyway.

Then he gave me a wink. My knees almost buckled at the sight.

Rather than putting his lips on mine again, Eric slowly walked me to the dance floor, pulling me as close as he could. He rested a hand on my back. I realized he wasn't shaking this time. He felt sure and steady.

"I missed you, too," he said in a soft tone. "More than you will ever know."

We danced to an instrumental version of "Dream a Little Dream of Me," a favorite of mine. I had a sudden thought that it would be a favorite of *ours* for years to come.

As we danced in slow, graceful movements, I rested my head on his welcoming shoulder. With closed eyes, I could feel Eric's heat radiating out through his suit. I slowly breathed in the spiciness of his cologne. It was almost hard to believe we'd never held each other like this before. It felt so comfortable, so natural. It was absolute perfection.

He guided me around the floor, and in those moments, I knew that the right guy found me. There never should have been a "Logan or Eric" debate. Eric had always been the one.

"Can we celebrate like this every day?" I asked him in a whisper, raising my head again. Our faces were so close that our noses almost touched. There was a twinkle in his eyes and a glow on his face that told me how happy he was. It was a happiness I knew would grow day after day, along with our deep, intense love for each other.

Eric kissed the palm of my hand that he held, his eyes the brightest shade of turquoise they'd ever been. "Always." He grinned.

Acknowledgements

First and foremost, I want to thank my husband for his love, support, encouragement, and patience throughout this journey. Thank you also to my son, family, and friends, who believed in me and encouraged me every step of the way. Extra heartfelt gratitude to Super Bestie Angie and Korey, without both of whom I might never have survived some of the most trying times of my life.

Special thanks to my incredibly talented and helpful editor, Joanne Lui, my amazing cover designer Brenda Camp Walter, and Paul Suggett for all the insightful information about copywriters and how advertising agencies work.

Many thanks to Josephine, Mary Ann, Katie, and Bec for your time and thoughtful opinions, and also to the awesome people who gave their helpful hints, however big or small, to aid me in this project.

Finally, thanks to all you readers out there who took a chance on me. I will be forever grateful!

About The Author

Though she grew up in a small town—or perhaps because she grew up there—Lisa Keifer always dreamed of living in the "big city."

Writing has always been a part of her in some form or another. Assignments in school, tales and plays she and her friends made up to amuse themselves, stories of her biggest dreams. However, it took her decades to realize just how important writing really was. Once this happened, there was no containing her desire to put pen to paper. Poetry, short stories, novels: she loved and still loves writing all three.

When not busy creating or revising, Lisa can often be found curled up on the sofa with a comfy blanket and—usually—heart-wrenching book. She occasionally attempts finishing a scrapbook she started years ago but doesn't seem to make much progress on. Lisa also loves spending time with her wonderful husband and adorable son, other family, friends, and their shop cat, Burt.